WHERE THERE'S LOVE, THERE'S HATE

ADOLFO BIOY CASARES (1914–99) was born into a wealthy family in Buenos Aires and wrote his first novella—for a cousin with whom he was in love—at the age of eleven. He published his first book, *Prólogo* (*Prologue*), just four years later. He met Jorge Luis Borges in 1932, beginning a lifelong friendship that produced many collaborations, including the invention of the mock detective Don Isidro Parodi. Also, through Borges's friend Victoria Ocampo he met his future wife: her sister, Silvina, whom he married in 1940. Bioy's most famous work is *The Invention of Morel* (1940), which inspired the film *Last Year at Marienbad*. He won many awards during his career, including the 1991 Cervantes Prize and the French Legion of Honor. He died in Buenos Aires in 1999.

SILVINA OCAMPO (1903–93) was born in Buenos Aires, the youngest of six siblings. As a young woman she traveled to Europe to pursue a career as a painter, studying under Giorgio de Chirico and Fernand Léger. She published her first work of fiction, the story collection *Forgotten Journey*, when she returned to Argentina in 1937. By this time she had begun a relationship with her future husband Adolfo Bioy Casares. She went on to publish several volumes of award-winning poetry, stories and children's books, and was twice awarded the Argentine National Literature Prize. With Borges and Bioy Casares she edited the groundbreaking 1940 *Anthology of Fantastic Literature*. She died in Buenos Aires in 1993.

SUZANNE JILL LEVINE has translated the work of Manuel Puig, Guillermo Cabrera Infante, and Jorge Luis Borges. Among her books is *The Subversive Scribe: Translating Latin American Fiction*.

JESSICA ERNST POWELL won a National Endowment for the Arts Fellowship for her translation of Antonio Benítez Rojo's *Woman in Battle Dress*.

THE NEVERSINK LIBRARY

I was by no means the only reader of books on board the
Neversink. *Several other sailors were diligent readers,
though their studies did not lie in the way of belles-lettres.
Their favourite authors were such as you may find at the
book-stalls around Fulton Market; they were slightly physiological in their nature. My book experiences on board of
the frigate proved an example of a fact which every book-
lover must have experienced before me, namely, that though
public libraries have an imposing air, and doubtless contain
invaluable volumes, yet, somehow, the books that prove
most agreeable, grateful, and companionable, are those we
pick up by chance here and there; those which seem put into
our hands by Providence; those which pretend to little, but
abound in much.* —HERMAN MELVILLE, *WHITE JACKET*

WHERE THERE'S LOVE, THERE'S HATE

ADOLFO BIOY CASARES AND SILVINA OCAMPO

TRANSLATED BY
SUZANNE JILL LEVINE AND
JESSICA ERNST POWELL

INTRODUCTION BY
SUZANNE JILL LEVINE

MELVILLE HOUSE PUBLISHING
BROOKLYN · LONDON

WHERE THERE'S LOVE, THERE'S HATE
Originally published as *Los Que Aman, Odian* by
Emecé Editores, Buenos Aires

Translation copyright © 2013, Suzanne Jill Levine and Jessica Ernst Powell

Design by Christopher King

First Melville House printing: March 2013

Melville House Publishing
145 Plymouth Street
Brooklyn, NY 11201

www.mhpbooks.com

ISBN: 978-1-61219-150-8

Manufactured in the United States of America
1 2 3 4 5 6 7 8 9 10

A catalog record for this title is available from the Library of Congress.

INTRODUCTION

BY SUZANNE JILL LEVINE

This quirky novella, originally published in 1946, is the only known work of fiction by Silvina Ocampo with her husband Adolfo Bioy Casares. *Where There's Love, There's Hate* (*Los Que Aman, Odian*, literally "Those Who Love, Hate") is a genre-bender, like so much of the better-known fiction of Bioy Casares: a tongue-in-cheek mystery somewhere between detective spoof and romantic satire.

In a remote seaside resort in Argentina infidelities engender "little murders" among the wealthy bourgeoisie and those who serve them, and in a tradition shared with Agatha Christie's *Then There Were None*, the reader begins to suspect every character. The principal narrator is Professor Huberman, portrayed as a self-involved pseudo-intellectual who fancies himself to be an amateur detective as well as a literary critic. He pontificates, "When will we at last renounce the detective novel, the fantasy novel and the entire prolific, varied, and ambitious literary genre that is fed by unreality? When will we return to the path of the salubrious picaresque and pleasant local color?" In the very first chapter he meets a wealthy couple who are writers—"dabblers in literature and fortunate with livestock"—an ironic wink at the couple writing this novella who were, indeed, devoted to "unreality."

It might be useful to consider this work an inevitable early offspring of Adolfo and Silvina's love of literary creation, shared humor, and often unconventional life together, as well as one of the many stories and book projects—including the groundbreaking 1940 *Antología de la literatura fantástica*—that came out of their conversations with their friend Jorge Luis Borges. In 1942 Borges and Bioy published their first collaborative detective fiction, *Six Problems for Don Isidro*, about a detective modeled after Poe's Auguste Dupin, who solves crimes—in parodic mode—from his jail cell. They took collaboration to another level, creating various fictional writers who produced a literary universe parallel to their individual creations. The Uruguayan literary critic and Yale scholar Emir Rodríguez Monegal referred to this third writer, who in some ways did not resemble either Bioy or Borges, as "Biorges." Aside from their collaborative fictions written under pseudonyms such as Bustos Domecq, they would also translate and publish an international detective series called *El septimo sello* or "The Seventh Seal."

It was in the summer of 1971 that I first met Adolfo Bioy Casares—called Bioy by friends and Adolfito by Silvina, family and those who knew him since childhood—though in the Southern Hemisphere it was a mild, sunny winter day. I was in Buenos Aires with my good friend, that same Emir Rodríguez Monegal, and his young colleague Alfred MacAdam. I was even

younger than Alfred, and this was a literary event for
both of us, entering the elegant Casares–Ocampo apart-
ment with its high ceilings and dark wooden shelves
lined with what seemed to be thousands of books from
floor to ceiling. A housemaid in uniform had opened
the door and led us silently from a shadowy foyer into
the book-lined salon.

We sat awaiting the writer who was already a legend
to us as readers as well as from Emir's anecdotes. The
saying goes (or went) that the Argentines speak Spanish like Italians, dine like Frenchmen, and dress like
Englishmen. This adage fit Bioy like a glove, except that
his speech was more "criollo"—native-born, that is,
more refined—unlike the Italianate of first or second-
generation immigrants who spoke the slang "lunfardo"
that Bioy and Borges would caricature in their collaborations. Bioy entered the room with a lively step: he was
strikingly handsome, rather slight, and looked athletic
despite his age—aside from his notable *donjuanismo*,
he had devoted himself to tennis in younger years.
(Apparently, I would later learn, he would often use
"tennis" as a pretext for amorous morning assignations
with willing young women.) His grayish white hair
was combed back neatly and under his thick eyebrows
twinkled smiling blue eyes; a strong, sensual mouth
countered the British elegance of his mien and attire.

As if a theatrical effect were being sought, Silvina
was the next to enter, jangling bracelets and graciously
offering us cocktails—that is, whiskey. In her slacks and
silk blouse Silvina was a striking apparition, a short,

sharp-featured woman in dark glasses who spoke with a notably nasal intonation. I often wondered, when later doing my first translation of Bioy's work—the comedic yet nightmarish satire *A Plan for Escape*—whether the nasal voice of a bizarre character in this novella were not inspired by Silvina's idiosyncratic upper-class Argentine speech.

I remember little from this initial meeting except that the conversation, a dialogue that had been interrupted some years back, was an intense and lively exchange of gossip, in-jokes and literary references—and that the experience of being there was magical, the Bioys' sitting room almost a timeless space of literature, like Melquiades's room in *One Hundred Years of Solitude*, but which is now ravaged by time, living in memory and in formerly lost objects like the novella we celebrate on this occasion.

That evening, or the next morning, Bioy called to invite Emir and me to dinner with Silvina and Borges, who often dined with them and whom I had met a year earlier on one of his lecture tours to the United States. That dinner is mentioned in the huge diary of Bioy's conversations with Borges from the 1940s through the 1980s, recently published in Spanish, in which Bioy's leitmotif throughout the book is "had dinner with Borges." This repeated notation was not an exaggeration: Borges, Bioy and Silvina would meet almost nightly in the forties and beyond, for dinner and to work on joint projects amongst and through the gossip and jokes. Hence, our evening with them had the added attraction of being included in their nightly ritual. Life has its highs, and those twelve days in Buenos Aires were certainly a zenith: with Emir I was meeting the crème de la crème of Argentina's literary life, including Tomas Eloy Martinez; the filmmaker Torre Nilsson and his spirited wife, the writer Beatriz Guido; the wonderfully poker-faced journalist Homero Alsina Thevenet, who could imitate Groucho Marx even better than Guillermo Cabrera Infante; the writer Pepe Bianco, who had been an editor of *Sur* magazine under the directorship of Victoria Ocampo; Hector Libertella; and Luisa Valenzuela and her mother Luisa Mercedes Levinson, to mention a few. I was in Buenos Aires on a literary mission of my own, working with Manuel Puig on the translation of his second novel, *Heartbreak Tango*. Now of course I look at these names and sadly observe how most of them, like Bioy and Silvina, are gone, inhabitants of an irretrievable past.

This irretrievable past is what urgently justifies our translation and publication now of this little book, precious in the present because it enriches our enjoyment and knowledge of that lost world, and nurtures our engagement with what Silvina considered yet another reason to write, that is, "not to forget what is most important in the world: friendship and love, wisdom and art."

It would require a microscopic reading to define the distinctive touches of each of these two authors that

combine to lend peculiar charm and style to this ec-
centric "mystery." Both writers were famous for surreal
whimsy, ironic dialogues, playful "Borgesian" erudition, private jokes, and a profound sense that to be
human is to be absurd. Silvina confessed, in her introduction to *Leopoldina's Dream*, a Penguin anthology of
her stories edited and translated by Daniel Balderston,
that she wrote both to explain herself and to forget, "to
find something others might find in Ovid in my un-
happiness or in my other self."

It is safe to say that among the many lines of investigation in the novella is the misplaced passion of a young
boy, a child, and this is certainly an element we might
consider to be Silvina's contribution. In the words of
scholar Fiona Mackintosh, Ocampo "fits quirkily into
the highly intellectual society of which she was part,
returning frequently to children or childlike characters
and making their world her world: she scrutinizes the
workings of nostalgia, demythifying childhood innocence, and proposes a flexible attitude to the perceived
boundaries between childhood and adulthood."

That flexibility regarding boundaries, which en-
abled both writers to liberate the child within, also
characterizes the fluid interplay of genre in Silvina's
own stories and Bioy's unique and prolific fictions.
Fantasy, romance, satire, parody, detective tales, science fiction—all these modes feed into the world of
Bioy Casares (most famously in *The Invention of Morel*,
but also in such fascinating novels as *A Plan for Escape*, *The Dream of Heroes*, *Asleep in the Sun*, and in *A*

Russian Doll and Other Stories), as do fantasy and satire in Silvina's stories, which are more perverse (and perhaps more "surreal" in the sense of inexplicable) than Bioy's. As Borges wrote about his dear friend Silvina in his preface to *Leopoldina's Dream,* "In Silvina Ocampo's stories there is something I have never understood: her strange taste for a certain kind of innocent and oblique cruelty; I attribute this to the interest, the astonished interest, that evil inspires in a noble soul."

While we could define Bioy and Silvina's narrative art from many points of view and with numerous terms, definitions are ultimately reductive, which is one reason I suppose why I have often returned to the ventriloquism of translation, which allows me to trace on a parallel path my engagement with a written work. The task of this translation has been made even more pleasurable by adding the element of collaboration with fellow translator Jessica Ernst Powell. Jessica and I first began this translation in my workshop at the University of California several years ago, and it has been an enjoyable odyssey into the challenges of the writing, working together to find the *mot juste*—and I gallicize here because, like many of their compatriots, Bioy and Silvina lived an identity more European than "third world," as Latin America was then categorized. Their ideal capital was Paris, *bien sûr*. And so, far from both Europe and Argentina, in this encapsulated paradise of Santa Barbara, both of us have brought to you in English the story of the murder at Bosque del Mar.

WHERE THERE'S
LOVE, THERE'S HATE

1

THE LAST DROPS OF ARSENIC (*ARSENICUM album*) dissolve in my mouth, insipidly, comfortingly. To my left, on the desk, I have a copy, a beautiful Bodoni, of Gaius Petronius' *Satyricon*. To my right, the fragrant tea tray, with its delicate chinaware and its nutritive jars. Suffice to say that the book's pages are well worn from innumerable readings; the tea is from China; the toast is crisp and delicate; the honey is from bees that have sipped from acacia flowers and lilacs. And so, in this encapsulated paradise, I shall begin to write the story of the murder at Bosque del Mar.

To my way of thinking, the first chapter begins in a dining car, on the night train to Salinas. Sharing my table were a couple who were friends of mine—dabblers in literature and fortunate with livestock—and a nameless young woman. Bolstered by the *consommé*, I explained my intentions: in search of a delectable and fruitful solitude—that is to say, in search of myself—I was on my way to the new seaside resort that the most refined nature enthusiasts amongst us had discovered: Bosque del Mar. I had cherished the idea of this trip for some time now, but the demands of the office—I belong, I must admit, to the brotherhood of Hippocrates—had postponed my vacation. The married couple reacted with interest to my frank declaration: although I was a respected physician—I invariably follow in the footsteps of Hahnemann—I also wrote screenplays, with varying degrees of success. Now, Gaucho Films, Inc. had commissioned me to write an adaptation of Petronius' tumultuous book, set in present-day Argentina. A seclusion at the beach was *de rigueur*.

We returned to our compartments. A short time later I was enveloped in thick railway blankets, my spirit still singing with the pleasurable sensation of having been understood. A sudden doubt tempered my joy: Had I acted rashly? Had I just handed, to that amateur couple, all the necessary elements to steal my ideas? I knew that it was useless to dwell on it. My spirit, ever malleable, sought refuge in the anticipated contemplation of the trees by the ocean. A pointless effort. I was still a night away from those pine groves... Like Betteredge with *Robinson Crusoe*, I resorted to my Petronius. With renewed admiration I read this paragraph:

> *This is the reason, in my opinion, why young men grow up such blockheads in the schools, because they neither see nor hear one single thing connected with the usual circumstances of everyday life, nothing but stuff about pirates lurking on the seashore with fetters in their hands, tyrants issuing edicts to compel sons to cut off their own fathers' heads, oracles in times of pestilence commanding three virgins or more to be sacrificed to stay the plague...*

The advice is still valid today. When will we at last renounce the detective novel, the fantasy novel and the entire prolific, varied, and ambitious literary genre that is fed by unreality? When will we return to the path of the salubrious picaresque and pleasant local color?

The sea air had begun to filter through the window. I closed it. I fell asleep.

2

FOLLOWING MY INSTRUCTIONS TO THE LETTER, the steward woke me at six in the morning. I performed a few brief ablutions with the remainder of the bottle of Villavicencio water that I had requested before retiring the night before, took ten drops of arsenic, dressed, and went to the dining car. My breakfast consisted of a fruit salad and two cups of *café con leche* (it's worth remembering: the tea on trains is from Ceylon). I was sorry not to have the opportunity to explain a few details of intellectual property law to the couple with whom I'd eaten dinner the previous evening; they were going much further than Salinas (known these days as Colonel Faustino Tambussi), and, undoubtedly intoxicated by the effects of an allopathic pharmacopoeia, they were giving over to sleep these liminal morning hours that are, thanks to our own indolence, the exclusive province of country folk.

Running nineteen minutes behind schedule—at 7:02—the train arrived in Salinas. No one assisted me with the luggage. The stationmaster—who was, as far as I could tell, the only person awake in the entire town— was too engrossed in a childish game of tossing wicker hoops with the engineer to help a solitary traveler, oppressed by time and luggage. At length he finished his dealings with the engineer and walked over to me. I am not a resentful person, and had already arranged my mouth in a friendly smile and was reaching for my hat, when, like a lunatic, he set upon the freight-car door. He opened it, lunged inside, and I saw five clamorous bird cages fall out into a heap on the platform. I was choked with indignation. I would gladly have offered to take charge of the hens in order to save them from such violence. I consoled myself with the thought that more merciful hands had wrestled with my suitcases.

I turned quickly toward the station's rear courtyard in order to confirm that the hotel car had arrived. It had not. Immediately, I decided to question the stationmaster. After looking for him for a while, I found him sitting in the waiting room.

"Are you looking for something?" he asked me.

I did not disguise my impatience.

"I am looking for you."

"Well, then, here I am."

"I am waiting for the car from the Hotel Central, in Bosque del Mar."

"If you don't mind a bit of company, I suggest that you take a seat. At least here there's a bit of a breeze." He consulted his watch. "It's 7:14 and already this hot. I'll be honest with you: this will end in a storm."

He took a small mother-of-pearl penknife from his pocket and began to clean his fingernails. I asked him if the hotel car would be much longer. He replied:

"My forecasts do not cover that issue."

He continued his work with the penknife.

"Where is the post office?" I asked.

"Go to the water pump, beyond the railcars on the dead-end track. Leaving the tree on your right-hand side, turn at a right angle, cross in front of Zudeida's house and don't stop until you get to the bakery. The tin hut is the post office." My informant traced the details of the trajectory in the air with his hands. Then he added: "If you find the guy in charge awake, I'll give you a prize."

I indicated where I'd left my luggage, begged him not to allow the hotel car to leave without me, and set forth into that wide-open labyrinth, under a blazing sun.

3

FEELING MUCH RELIEVED BY THE PRECISE instructions I had given—all correspondence in my name should be forwarded to the hotel—I embarked on my return. I stopped at the water pump, and, after some rather vigorous exertion, I managed to stave off my thirst and to wet my head with two or three splashes of tepid water. Proceeding unsteadily, I arrived at the station.

In front sat an old Rickenbacker, loaded with the chicken cages. How much longer would I be forced to wait in this inferno for the hotel's car to collect me?

In the waiting room I found the stationmaster speaking with a man in a thick leather jacket. The man asked me:

"Doctor Humberto Huberman?"

I nodded. The stationmaster said:

"We'll load your luggage now."

It is incredible how much happiness these words afforded me. Without too much trouble I managed to settle in among the chicken cages. We began our journey toward Bosque del Mar.

The first fifteen miles of the road consisted of a series of potholes; the admirable Rickenbacker progressed slowly and hazardously. I looked for the sea, like a Greek advancing on Troy: not a single trace of purity in the air seemed to announce its proximity. Clustered around a water trough, a flock of sheep tried to find shelter from the sun in the feeble strips of shade cast by a windmill. My traveling companions stirred in their cages. Each time the car came to a stop at a gate, a dusting of feathers, like flower pollen, would spread through the air, and an ephemeral olfactory sensation would remind me of a happy episode from my childhood, with my parents in my uncle's henhouses in Burzaco. Might I confess that for a few moments I took refuge, in the midst of the jostling and the heat, in the pristine vision of a boiled egg set in a white porcelain teacup?

At last we came to a range of sand dunes. In the distance I made out a crystalline fringe. I greeted the sea: *Thalassa!... Thalassa!...* It was a mirage. Forty minutes later I saw a wine-dark expanse. Inwardly, I yelled: *Epi oinopa ponton!* I turned to the chauffeur.

"This time I am not mistaken. There is the sea."

"It's a field of purple flowers," he replied.

A short while later, I noted that the potholes had ceased. The chauffeur told me:

"We must move quickly. The tide comes up in a few hours."

I looked around. We were advancing slowly over some thick planks, in the middle of a stretch of sand. The sea appeared in the distance, between the sand dunes to the right. I asked:

"Well, then, why are you going so slowly?"

"If a tire goes off the planks, the sand will bury us."

I did not want to think about what would happen were we to encounter another automobile. I was too tired to worry. I didn't even notice the cool marine air. I managed to formulate the question:

"Are we nearly there?"

"No," he replied. "Twenty-five miles."

4

I AWOKE IN THE DARK. I DIDN'T KNOW
where I was or what time it was. I strained to orient
myself. I remembered: I was in my room at the Hotel
Central. Then I heard the ocean.

I turned on the light and saw by my timepiece—on
the pine nightstand amid the volumes by Chiron, Kent,
Jahr, Allen, and Hering—that it was five o'clock in the
evening. Sluggishly, I began to get dressed. What a relief to be freed of the rigorous attire that the conven-
tionality of urban life imposes upon us! Like a fugitive
from clothing, I sheathed myself in my Scottish shirt,
flannel pants, raw-canvas jacket, foldable Panama hat,
old yellow clodhoppers, and my walking cane with the
handle in the shape of a dog's head. I tilted my head
and, with barefaced admiration, studied my protruding
thinking-man's forehead: once again I had to concur
with so many an impartial observer that the likeness
between my facial features and Goethe's was authen-
tic. As for the rest of me, I am not a tall man; to use
an evocative term, I am pocket-sized—my moods, my
reactions and my thoughts neither extend nor blunt
themselves over a distended geography. I am proud of
my mane of hair, pleasing to both sight and touch, of
my small and beautiful hands, and of my slender wrists,

ankles and waist. My feet—"frivolous travelers"—do not rest even when I am asleep. My complexion is soft and pink; my appetite, perfect.

I made haste. I wanted to take full advantage of my first day at the beach.

Like those long-forgotten memories we recall only later when we come across them in a photo album, the moment that I loosened the straps on my suitcase I saw—for the first time?—the scenes of my arrival at the hotel. The building, white and modern, appeared picturesquely set in the sand like a ship on the sea, or an oasis in the desert. The scarcity of trees was compensated by some random green blotches—dandelions that seemed to advance like a multiplying reptile, and the murmuring stalks of tamarisk shrubs. In the distance were two or three houses and a few huts.

I was no longer tired. I felt a kind of jubilant ecstasy. I, Doctor Humberto Huberman, had discovered the literati's paradise. In two months of working in this solitude I would finish my adaptation of Petronius. And then... *A new heart, a new man.* The moment to seek out other authors, to renew my spirit, will have arrived at last.

I moved stealthily along darkened passageways. I wanted to avoid any possible conversation with the hotel's owners—distant relatives of mine—that would have delayed my encounter with the sea. I had the good fortune to slip outside without being seen and to begin my trek across the sand. It was a difficult peregrination. City life weakens and enervates us to such an extent that, in the shock of the first moment, the simple pleasures of the countryside become a torture. Nature wasted no time in persuading me of the inadequacy of my attire. With one hand I pressed my hat to my head so that the wind would not snatch it from me, and with the other I sank my cane into the sand, futilely seeking the stability of the planks that surfaced, every so often, to mark the path. My shoes, filled with sand, were but further hindrances to my progress.

At last I came to an area of more firmly packed sand. Some two hundred feet to the right, a gray sailboat lay in the sand; I saw that a rope ladder hung from the deck over the side, and I told myself that on one of my next walks I would climb it and explore the boat. Closer to the sea, next to a stand of tamarisk shrubs, a pair of or-ange umbrellas fluttered in the wind. Emerging against a backdrop of an unbelievably bright sea and sky, in sharp focus as though seen through a lens, were two girls in bathing suits and a man in a blue captain's hat with the legs of his trousers rolled up.

There was nowhere else to take shelter from the wind. I decided to move closer to the tamarisks, behind the beach umbrellas.

I took off my shoes and socks and stretched out on the sand. A perfect sensation of pleasure. Almost perfect: it was tempered by the thought of my inevi-table return to the hotel. In order to avoid any intru-sion by the neighbors—in addition to the three already mentioned, there was another man hidden by an um-brella—I turned to my Petronius and pretended to be engrossed in my reading. But, in truth, my only reading in those moments of irremissible abandon was, like a vision or an omen, the white flight of seagulls against a leaden sky.

What I had not foreseen when I settled close to the umbrellas was that their occupants would be talking. They spoke without the slightest regard for the beauty of the afternoon or for their weary neighbor who was trying, in vain, to lose himself in his reading. The voices, which until then had mingled with the chorus of the sea and the cry of the gulls, were now disagreeably clear and distinct. I thought I recognized at least one of the female voices.

Moved by a natural curiosity, I turned toward the group. I did not at first see the girl whose voice I thought I had recognized; she was hidden behind an umbrella. Her companion was standing: she was tall and blonde and—dare I say—quite beautiful, with strikingly pale skin and pink cheeks ("the color of raw salmon," as Doctor Manning would later declare). Her body was too athletic for my taste and, like a tacit presence, she exuded an animal magnetism that attracts certain types of men about whose inclinations I prefer not to comment.

After listening to their conversation for a few minutes I had collected the following facts: the blonde girl, named Emilia, was a dangerous music-lover. The other girl, Mary, translated and edited detective novels for a prestigious publishing house. Two men accompanied them. One of them—in the blue cap—was a Doctor Cornejo; I was impressed by his good-natured manner and his intimate knowledge of the ocean and of meteorology. He must have been about fifty years old; his gray hair and thoughtful eyes lent him a romantic air, not without vigor. The other man was younger, and of a darker complexion. Despite a certain vulgarity in his manner of speech and an appearance that brought to mind the posters for *Tango à Paris*—straight black hair, sparkling eyes, aquiline nose—he seemed to exert over his companions—none too brilliant, in any event—a certain intellectual superiority. I discovered that his name was Enrique Atuel and that he was Emilia's fiancé.

"It's too late for you to go swimming, Mary," he said, in an even tone. "And besides, the ocean is rough and you don't handle the undercurrent too well."

The voice that I recognized rang out happily: "This girl is going swimming!"

"You're a brat," replied Emilia, affectionately. "Are you trying to kill yourself or just hoping to scare the rest of us to death?"

Emilia's fiancé was insistent: "You can't go swimming with the current like this, Mary. It would be crazy."

Cornejo consulted his wristwatch.

"The tide is coming in," he pronounced. "There is no danger whatsoever. If you promise not to go too far, you have my consent."

Atuel addressed the girl:

"If you can't get back in, his consent won't do you a bit of good. Take my advice and don't go in."

"To the water!" shouted Mary, gleefully.

She jumped up, adjusted her swim cap and said: "I am a girl with wings! I am a girl with wings!"

"In that case, I want nothing more to do with this," said Atuel. "I'm going back."

"Don't be silly," Emilia said to him.

Atuel walked off, ignoring her. As he was leaving he discovered my presence and gave me a stern look. For my part, I admit that I was captivated by Mary's graceful body. It was true: she was a girl with wings. At each wave she raised her arms high above her head, as though playing with the sky.

"Mary? Miss María Gutiérrez?" I wondered. It is so difficult to recognize people in their bathing suits... The young woman whom I had seen earlier this year in my office and to whom I recommended a vacation in Bosque del Mar? Yes, I was sure of it. That young woman delicately lost in a fur coat. There were the same dark eyes, by turns mischievous and dreamy. There was the cowlick on her forehead. I remembered that I had said to her, good-naturedly: "We are kindred spirits." As with me, her case called for arsenic. There she was, jumping up and down in the ocean, the very same girl who had lain, sick, upon the comfortable cushions in my office. Another miraculous cure by Doctor Huberman!

I was startled out of my reverie by some anxious shouts. In point of fact, the famous swimmer had gotten very far out with extraordinary ease.

"She swam out there in grand form," observed Cornejo in a calming tone. "She's in no danger. She'll be back."

"She's that far out because the current carried her," declared Emilia.

Hearing someone shouting, I turned my head to look.

"She can't get back in!"

It was Atuel, coming towards us and gesticulating wildly. He confronted Cornejo face to face:

"Did you get what you wanted? She can't get back in."

I deemed it high time for me to intervene. In truth, it was a perfect opportunity for me to practice the crawl and the life-saving skills—so easily forgotten—that Professor Chimmara at the Health Department had imparted to me.

"Gentlemen," I said resolutely, "if someone will lend me a bathing suit, I will rescue her."

"That is an honor I reserve for myself," declared Cornejo. "But perhaps we can indicate to her that she should swim at an angle, in a north to southeasterly direction..."

Atuel interrupted him:

"At an angle, what rubbish! The girl is drowning."

An instinctive movement, or else the desire to avoid witnessing a fight, turned my gaze in the direction of the boat. I saw a boy climb down the rope ladder and come running toward us.

Atuel was getting undressed. Cornejo and I were arguing over a pair of swim trunks.

The boy was screaming:

"Emilia! Emilia!"

Before our astonished eyes, Emilia ran down the beach, swam out to Mary, returned with Mary.

Joyfully, we surrounded the swimmers. Slightly pale, Mary looked more beautiful than ever. With forced nonchalance she said:

"You are all a bunch of alarmists. That's what you are: alarmists."

Doctor Cornejo tried to persuade her:

"When the water is whipped up by the wind, you shouldn't let it hit you in the face."

The boy was still crying. To console him, Mary put her beautiful wet arms around him. She said tenderly:

"Did you think I was drowning, Miguel? I am the girl of the sea and the waves and I have a secret."

Mary was demonstrating, as always, her exquisite grace, but she also revealed a dark vanity and that fatal ingratitude of swimmers who never admit to the danger they had been in and who dismiss those who have rescued them.

Among the characters in this episode there was one who made a vivid impression on me. It was the boy— the son of Andrea, the hotel owner's sister. He looked to be about eleven or twelve years old. His expression was quite noble; the lines of his face were even and well defined; nonetheless, his face also revealed a mixture of maturity and innocence I found unpleasant.

"Doctor Huberman!" exclaimed Mary, surprised. She had recognized me.

Chatting amiably, we headed back. I looked toward the hotel. It was a small white cube against a sky of boldly twisting grey clouds. I thought of a catechism image from my childhood, entitled "The Divine Wrath."

5

HOW ADMIRABLY AND OBEDIENTLY A BODY
not tainted by allopathic medicine responds! With just
a simple glass of cold cocoa my fatigue vanished. I felt
emboldened, ready to face any and all vicissitudes that
life might send my way. I had a brief moment of doubt.
Wouldn't it be better to use routine as my ally and begin
my literary endeavors right then and there? Or could
I wholly devote this first afternoon of vacation to re-
storative leisure? For an instant, my respectful hands
caressed the Petronius. I gazed at it nostalgically, and
then set it on the bedside table.

Before leaving I tried to open the window so that
the afternoon air would sweep through my room. Resolutely, I grasped the handle. I turned it and gave the
requisite tug... I threw myself against the window. It
was impossible to open.

This amusing incident brought to mind my Aunt
Carlota's well-known eccentricities. She also owned a
beachside property, in Necochea, and she was so afraid
of the effect that the sea air might have on metal objects that she had ordered the house built with false
windows and, when there were no guests, she would
wrap everything in rolls of paper, from the handle on

the phonograph to the chain in the water closet. From the looks of it, this was a sort of family mania that had extended out to the furthest and least reputable of our line. But I was determined that they would open the window for me—using tools, if necessary—in order to refresh the air that was fouling my room. Already, I felt a headache coming on.

I had to speak with the hotel owners. Groping my way along the darkened hallways, where the air was as dense as it was in my room, I advanced until I came to a gray concrete staircase. I wavered between going up or down. Following my first impulse, I went down. The air became even more suffocating. I found myself in a curious basement. There was a kind of foyer, with a counter and a cabinet for keys. A room on the other side of a glass door was stocked with canned foods, bottles of wine, and cleaning products. On one of the walls, an enormous fresco displayed a mysteriously moving scene: in a room decorated with palms, in front of a large, wide-open window through which flooded a splendid sunlight, a boy, who looked like a small page, leaned gently toward a dead girl laid out on a bed. I wondered who the anonymous painter might be. The girl's face shone with an angelic beauty, while the boy's face, owing to powers that seemed unrelated to the art of painting, revealed vast measures of both intelligence and pain. But perhaps I was mistaken; I am not an art critic (although everything cultural, when it doesn't stifle my life, falls within my purview).

I tried to open the glass door, but it was locked. At

that moment I heard shouts. They seemed to be coming from another floor. Moved by an uncontrollable curiosity, I ran up the stairs. I paused on the landing, gasping for breath. I heard the screams again, coming from the left side at the end of the hallway. Cautiously, I crept forward. Something swift and amorphous fled past, brushing against my arm. Trembling (I felt as if I'd just been charged by a phantasmagorical cat), I followed the fleeing shadow with my eyes. The uncertain light from the staircase window provided me with a revelation: the little snoop was Miguel, the boy I had met that afternoon on the beach! I would be certain to reprimand him at the first opportunity. I set out toward my room at the other end of the hall, but by now it was impossible not to hear the voices. Reluctantly, I strained to place them. They were the voices from the beach. Emilia and Mary were insulting one another with a shocking ferocity! I could scarcely bear to listen to them. I retreated, profoundly unsettled.

I returned to my room (still shut tight), and opened my medicine kit, which gleamed with white labels and brown and green vials. I put the ten drops of arsenic onto a clean sheet of paper, and let them fall onto my tongue. It was exactly fifteen minutes until dinnertime.

6

MY APPETITE WAS PERFECTLY SATISFACTORY.
I deemed it prudent to arrive in the dining area five
minutes prior to dinnertime so as not to be caught
offguard by the dinner bell. I found my relatives, the
hotel's owners, busily distributing napkins and bread-
baskets. I decided, without further ado, to broach the
subject of my window. I was not a paying guest at the
hotel—my relatives owed me, from time immemorial, a
certain quantity of money—but I was not well disposed
to being treated as one who receives favors. My cousin,
a none too sanguine man, prematurely gray, with large,
pensive eyes and a tired expression, listened with equanimity, almost tenderness, to my order that the window
be unstuck immediately. A solicitous silence was his
sole reaction. Andrea, his wife, interjected:

"What did I tell you, Esteban? We are being buried in sand here. Anywhere you turn, there is sand; it's
infinite."

A sudden enthusiasm came over Esteban.

"That's not true, Andrea. To the south, there are
crabs. On October 23rd of last year, no, it was the 24th,
the pharmacist's horse got stuck in the marsh; he disappeared into the mud before our very eyes."

"I liked that parcel in Claromecó," continued Andrea,

with perverse resentment. "But Esteban wouldn't hear of it. And here we are, in debt, in this hotel that only brings in expenses."

Andrea was young and healthy, with lively eyes and regular features, but not at all good-looking. Her boundless resentment manifested itself in overwrought and aggressive amiability.

Esteban said, "When we first arrived, there was nothing here except a little tin hut, the sea, and the sand. Now, there's our hotel, the New East End Hotel, and the pharmacy. The tamarisks have finally taken root. I realize that this is a slow season, but last year, all of the rooms were filled. The place is making progress."

"Perhaps I have not expressed myself clearly," I said, ironically. "What I want is for you to open my window."

"Impossible," replied Andrea with irritating calm. "Just ask Esteban. What progress? Two years ago, our lobby was on the first floor; now it's the basement. The sand rises constantly. If we opened your window, the house would fill up with sand."

The window was a lost cause. I am—at least on the surface—a good loser. In order to change the subject I begged my cousins to tell me what they knew about the sailboat foundered in the sand that I had seen during my afternoon walk. Esteban replied:

"It's the *Joseph K*. It came in with the tide one night. When we first settled here there was another boat as well, but a storm came up and, from one day to the next, the sea carried it off."

"My nephew," said Andrea, "plays in that boat for

hours. It's a mystery to me that he doesn't get bored. What could he be doing there, all alone, all day long?"

"It's not a mystery to me," replied Esteban. "That boat makes me wish I were a kid again."

The gong of the dinner bell interrupted our conversation. A fat old woman was beating upon it zealously, smiling like a simpleton. They told me that she was the typist.

The guests didn't take long to arrive. We sat marooned at one end of an excessively long table. I was introduced to the only person I had not yet met: Doctor Manning. He was small, pink-faced, wrinkled and taciturn. He was dressed as a fisherman and had a pipe permanently stuck in his mouth, covering him in ashes.

One chair was empty: Emilia was missing.

Andrea, assisted by a servant, served the table. Esteban ate listlessly. We had finished the pea soup when he stood with deliberate calm, went over to the radio, put on his eyeglasses, moved the dials, and deafened us with a bolero.

Somewhat insistently, I shot glances of admonition and reproach at the boy, Miguel. He avoided my gaze and stared, with feigned interest, at Mary. Doctor Cornejo was looking at her too.

"What beautiful rings!" exclaimed Cornejo, taking the girl's hand firmly in his own. "The bands are fourteen carat and the rubies are perfect."

"Yes, they're not bad," replied Mary. "I inherited them. My mother put all her money in precious jewels."

I confess that, at first, Mary's gems seemed more

like costume jewels than the genuine article. There are, to be sure, similarities between modern baubles and the finest of ancient jewels—the color of the stones, the complexity of the settings, the symbolism of the design—that disorient the casual observer. My cousin, the hotel owner, did not appear to share in this confusion. Greed gleamed in her eyes.

Raising my voice excessively—the radio conspired against us—I asked Mary what interesting books she had read of late.

"Oh!" she responded. "The only books I read are those I translate. I'll have you know that they make up a respectable library."

"I hadn't judged you to be such a hard worker," I remarked.

"If you don't believe me, go up to my room," she said in a sarcastic tone. "There I have all the books I have translated. Why is it that I can't be without my things? I love them so! . . . I also keep the manuscripts of the translations and the rough drafts of the manuscripts!"

We were on to the second course—some fowl a bit too tender for my taste—when Emilia arrived. Her eyes were shiny and red, as though she had just been crying. She had that fragile and solemn air of isolation of one who has been weeping. There was a general sense of unease, undiminished by each of our efforts to dispel it.

Mary asked us: "Would it bother you if I turned off the radio?"

"We'd be grateful," I replied, politely.

The silence was a relief, but not a lasting one. With

the music silenced, we now had nowhere to hide, and each of us was a shameless witness to the discomfort of the others and to the tragedy of Emilia. What secret enmity burned in that girl's heart? A treatise remains to be written about the weeping of women; what one believes to be an expression of tenderness is, at times, an expression of hatred, and the sincerest of tears tend to be spilled by women who are moved only by their own predicaments.

With excellent pluck, Doctor Cornejo tried to re-animate the conversation. Aided by diagrams he traced with a fork on the tablecloth, he explained the complete tidal system of the South Atlantic coast. Then, to my cousins' increasing alarm, he proceeded to design two improbable breakwaters for our beach. He went on to speak of the crab bogs, and modeled the positions, quite realistically, that we should assume in the event we were to fall into one.

At last we were beginning to forget about Emilia when Mary intervened:

"Oh, I'm as worried as Santa Lucía! The sand has made Emilia's eyes look as though she's been crying." She turned to her sister. "Come by my room afterwards and I'll lend you some eye drops."

The delicacy with which Mary tried to disguise her sister's crying was admirable. The latter didn't even respond.

But Mary thought of everything.

Unlike half of humanity, she remembered that it was offensive to prescribe anything—even a few drops of *aqua fortis*—in the presence of a doctor. She exclaimed with her habitual grace:

"How silly of me, with a doctor present! Why don't you take a quick look at my sister? What harm could it do?"

I put on my glasses and looked intensely at Emilia. I asked her deferentially:

"Do you have headaches after reading? Do you feel a burning in those pretty little eyes, like two balls of flame? Do you see flies that aren't there? Do you see a green halo encircling lamps at night? Do your lachrymal ducts dilate when exposed to air?"

I interpreted her silence as an affirmative. I determined on the spot:

"*Ruta foetida*, one thousand. Ten drops upon waking. I have some vials in my medicine kit. If you'll allow me, I'll give you one."

"Thank you, Doctor. That won't be necessary," replied Emilia. She seemed not to notice my attentions. She went on:

"It's not the sand that made me cry."

These words did nothing to dampen the intensity of the circumstances.

Doctor Cornejo, that vigorous volunteer, intervened:

"I have been summering at the coast for twenty years now, the last eight of them in Quequén. And so, my friends, I can assure you that there's no beach more attractive than this for the study of the shifting of sand."

He went on to lay out the plans, on the tablecloth, for a future plantation, intended to fix down the sand dunes. In the face of such determined fork strokes, my cousin Andrea began to tremble.

Doctor Manning retired to a distant table with the last of the grapes. I saw him take a miniature deck of cards from his pocket and begin to play game after game of solitaire.

"I can't go for one day without hearing music," said Mary, looking oddly at her sister.

"Would you like me to turn on the radio?" inquired Atuel.

"What? With a soloist present?" exclaimed Mary, revealing new proof of her extraordinary sensitivity. She approached her sister and, taking her by the arm, implored her with an affectionate expression:

"Play something from your repertoire, Emilia."

She answered: "I don't feel like it."

"Don't be that way, Emilia," encouraged her fiancé. "The guests want to hear you."

I deemed it the right moment to intervene.

"I am certain," I said slowly and deliberately, "that the young lady won't deny us the honor of hearing her play."

Finally, Emilia had to accede. With poorly masked irritation, she was moving towards the piano, when Mary interrupted her.

"Emilia," she said, "you should play the *Forgotten Waltz*, by Liszt."

The pianist froze, staring rigidly at Mary. I thought I detected in her eyes, blue and diaphanous, the frigidity of hatred. Then, suddenly, her features calmed.

"I'm not in the mood to play such a happy piece," she replied with indifference. "I'd prefer Debussy's *Clair de lune*."

"The *Clair de lune* does not suit your sensibilities. Your hands play it, but your soul is absent. The waltz, Emilia, the waltz."

"The waltz!" I exclaimed, gallantly.

I do not consider myself an expert in musical matters, but I understood that it would strike the correct tone to support Mary's motion.

Atuel interrupted:

"Poor Emilia! They won't let her play what she wants."

This sentence was an unjustifiable act of aggression against me. I let it go. I saw that Emilia was looking at Atuel with tears in her eyes.

Mary insisted on her request. Emilia shrugged her shoulders, sat down at the piano, thought for a few moments, and began to play. Mary's critique had been justified: Emilia's technique was more in evidence than her soul. The execution was, partially, correct; but one noted unfortunate hesitations, as though the pianist had forgotten, or never really knew, the piece she was performing. We all applauded. With a tenderness that moved me, Mary kissed her sister. Then she exclaimed:

"How well Adriana Sucre played that piece!"

Perhaps to erase the poor impression she'd left, Emilia launched, with lucid enthusiasm, into the crystalline chords of the *Melancholy Waltz*. But only the ancient typist was listening. The rest of us preferred to listen to the delicious childhood anecdotes that the music inspired so fortuitously in Mary. I can safely say that the two brief oral biographies Mary outlined for us—her, spoiled and adorable; Emilia, more ironic but equally affectionate—were works of art comparable, in their respective genre, to the music of Liszt. Emilia finished playing. Mary cried out to her:

"I was just telling these gentlemen about how our mother always favored you! Whenever one of your boyfriends would arrive, she would ask the piano instructor to play, and later would make them believe that it had been you playing all along. You should have used the same strategy today, for the *Forgotten Waltz*."

"You're right," answered Emilia, "but don't forget that I didn't want to play it. And anyway, I don't know why you insist on being so aggressive with me."

Mary cried pathetically:

"Wicked! That's what you are: a wicked girl." She started to sob.

Atuel addressed Emilia:

"It's true. You are heartless," he told her.

We all surrounded Mary (except Doctor Manning who continued, drearily and distractedly, losing at solitaire). Mary cried like a girl, like a little princess (as Cornejo observed). Seeing her so pained and so beautiful served to prove to me—I say this selfishly—that *I for one* did have a heart. We were so busy with Mary that no one noticed that Emilia had retired, except perhaps little Miguel, who watched us, captivated, as though we were acting out a scene from the Grand Guignol.

Doctor Cornejo, in whom I was beginning to notice a decided inclination toward meddling in the affairs of others, proposed that one of us go in search of Emilia.

"No," said Atuel, with unaccustomed good sense. "It's best to leave hysterical women alone. Isn't that the case, Doctor?"

I conceded the point.

Outside, the dogs took turns howling. The old woman who served as the typist went to the window. Smiling blankly, she exclaimed:

"What a night! What dogs! They barked this way when Grandpa died. We were at a beautiful seaside resort, just as we are now."

She continued moving her head, as though still hearing music.

Suddenly, the howling of the dogs was drowned out by an immense moan; it was as if a gigantic, supernatural dog, out on the deserted beaches, were grieving all the world's sorrow. The wind had come up.

"A windstorm. We must close the doors and windows," declared my cousin.

A drumming sound, like rain, beat against the walls.

"Here it rains sand," noted my cousin. Then she added: "Just as long as we don't end up buried..."

Nimbly, the rotund typist closed the windows. She looked at us, smiling, and said: "Something is going to happen tonight! Something is going to happen tonight!"

Doubtlessly, these unsolicited words had a moving effect on Mary's emotional soul.

"Where could Emilia be?" she asked, forgetting all resentment. "I demand that someone go and look for her."

"I'll overlook the demand, so no one will accuse me of weakness," conceded Atuel. "Perhaps Doctor Cornejo would like to accompany me. . ."

The urgent howling of the wind outside contrasted with the scant still air inside, where we were suffocating together, gathered around a steadfast lamp. The wait seemed interminable.

Finally, the men returned.

"We've looked everywhere," affirmed Cornejo. "She has disappeared."

Mary broke into a new crying jag. We decided to ready ourselves for a rescue mission. We all ran off to our respective rooms in search of overcoats. I also out-fitted myself in a wool cap, a plaid jacket and fur-lined gloves. I wrapped a Scottish scarf about my neck. I did not forget the magic lantern.

I was already on my way out when I remembered my medicine kit. I removed a vial of *Ruta foetida*—the inspiration of a worldly man.

"Here, take this," I said to Mary, when I returned to the dining room. "Give it to your sister, tomorrow."

This calm declaration had a radical effect on Mary. Too radical, in my opinion: minutes later, as I was head-ing towards the hotel's exit, I saw, against the whiteness of the wall, two shadows kissing. It was Atuel and Mary. But I wish to be clear: Atuel was resisting; Mary was besieging him passionately.

"What are we," I murmured, "but skeletons kissed by the gods?" With a heavy soul I continued on my way. Something cried out in the dark. It was the boy. I had stumbled over him. He looked at me for a moment— what was in his expression: contempt, hatred, terror?— and then he fled.

Four men, struggling, scarcely managed to push open the door. We found ourselves out in the night. The wind tried to knock us to the ground and the sand whipped us in the face, blinding us.

"This is not letting up," my cousin predicted.

We split up in search of the lost girl.

7

BY THE NEXT MORNING, MARY WAS DEAD. I was awakened shortly before eight by an unpleasant noise: it was Andrea calling me, asking for help. I turned on the light, jumped quickly out of bed, with a steady hand deposited the ten drops of arsenic onto the paper and transferred them to my tongue, wrapped myself in my purple *robe de chambre*, and opened the door. Andrea looked at me with weepy eyes, as if preparing to throw herself into my arms. I kept my hands resolutely in my pockets.

I soon learned what had happened. As I followed her through the halls of the hotel, my cousin told me that Emilia had just discovered her sister, dead. I extracted the information through a dense weft of sobs and whimpers.

I had a melancholy premonition. I thought of my promised vacation, my literary endeavors. I murmured, "Farewell, Petronius," and delved into the room of the tragedy.

My first impression was a tender one: the lamp illuminating Emilia's head against a row of books. She was crying soundlessly, and I seemed to detect a peacefulness in her beautiful face that I had not noticed before. On the table was a pile of manuscripts and proofs; a warm burst of sympathy throbbed in my chest. The dead girl was in the bed and, at first glance, appeared to be sleeping peacefully. I looked at her more closely: she displayed signs of strychnine poisoning.

Emilia asked, in a voice sobbing with hope, "Could it be an epileptic fit?"

I would have loved to have been able to answer in the affirmative. I allowed my silence to answer for me.

"A fainting spell?" asked Andrea.

Atuel entered the room. The others—from my cousin Esteban to the typist, even Manning and Cornejo—were crowded at the door.

I judged that the death had occurred within the last two hours. In response to Andrea's question I said:

"She was poisoned."

"I pay close attention to the food I serve my guests," replied Andrea, offended. "If it had been something she ate, we would all be..."

"I am not saying that she ingested tainted food. She ingested poison."

Doctor Cornejo entered the room, opened his arms and addressed me, impetuously:

"But Doctor, what are you suggesting? How dare you, in front of Miss Emilia...?"

I adjusted my glasses and gazed at Doctor Cornejo with impassive disdain. His affected courtesy, a mere pretext to interfere, was beginning to try my patience. Further, between his excitement and his gesticulating, he was panting like a gymnast. The room lacked air.

I responded dryly:

"The dilemma is clear: suicide or murder."

My words made a profound impression. I went on:

"Nevertheless, clearly, I am not the doctor who will issue the death certificate... You should all try to convince *him* that this is a suicide."

I myself could probably have been convinced of it rather quickly. But my words were the offspring of passion: it amused me to fluster Cornejo. Besides, with that plural—"you should all"—I was putting everyone present under suspicion for murder. I found this amusing as well.

"I'm afraid that Doctor Huberman is correct—" affirmed Atuel, and I remembered his shadow, and Mary's. He went on:

"Here is the vial of drops that she took every morning; the stopper is on the floor... If the poison was hidden in there, we find ourselves faced with a crime."

It was the last straw; we could no longer avoid involving the police. It occurred to me that, in the future, I might do better to control my impulses.

Doctor Cornejo declared:

"Do not forget that we are among gentlemen. I refuse to accept your conclusions."

A scream, harrowing and primordial, interrupted my musings. Then I heard the sound of hurried steps, moving away from us.

"What was that?" I asked.

"Miguel," came the reply.

The boy's intemperate outburst seemed a reproach to us all, for having indulged in petty spite in the face of the undeniable miracle of death.

8

THE STORM HAD ABATED. WE SENT THE Rickenbacker to Salinas.

Emilia and Atuel had sat with the body throughout the morning. The rest of the guests discreetly took turns performing that sad duty. Andrea scarcely appeared in the room. The fact that someone had died in her hotel vexed her; to now have to receive the police and face an investigation was something that exceeded her limits of understanding and tolerance. She was careless in her interactions with Atuel and Emilia. She did not disguise her resentment when speaking of the deceased.

At eleven on the dot I approached the kitchen to ask Andrea to prepare my habitual broth with toast points. I was met with a disagreeable sight: Andrea was pale and a tremble in her jaw foretold the imminence of a sob. Barely hiding my impatience, I realized that a delay in the arrival of my soup was all but inevitable. I decided it would be prudent not to speak until it had been served.

While I am disposed to noting my cousin's many faults, I must admit that she is an excellent cook. The soup she brought me was perhaps superior even to the one my two jovial dwarfs prepare for me at the office.

Straddling the carpenter's bench with the tray in front of me, I resigned myself to listening to Andrea.

"I'm worried about Miguel," she assured me, in a tone that seemed to suggest that the two of us alone were in possession of good sense and equanimity. "Those women forget that he is only a boy and they make no attempt to shield him from their arguments or carryings on with their boyfriends."

The elderly typist passed fleetly by, a flyswatter in her hand. Presently, I heard the monotonous blows that the huntress unleashed upon the walls and furniture. Since the storm made opening the windows impossible, the hotel was full of flies. The atmosphere was oppressive.

"You are forgetting that one of 'those women' has died," I said, picking up the conversation with Andrea.

It wasn't only the soup that deserved high praise. The toast was outstanding.

"They'll have driven him completely mad with all that. I'm worried, Humberto. Miguel has had a sad childhood. He's anemic, poorly developed. He's quite small for his age. He broods all the time. My brother thought that the ocean could bolster him up... He's in his room crying. I would like you to go see him."

My cousin's cruelty toward the deceased should not have muddled my thinking; what she had said about the boy hit the nail on the head. First impressions leave an imprint on the soul that reverberates throughout one's life. It is incumbent upon all men that this echo not be ominous. I could not forget, however, Miguel's disagreeable attitude, eavesdropping on Emilia and Mary's private quarrels.

I followed Andrea into the depths of the hotel, into a storage room full of trunks among which they had placed a bed for Miguel. While I groped along the walls, searching in vain for the light switch, Andrea lit a match. Then she lit the stub of a candle, stuck in a light-blue candlestick set atop one of the trunks.

The boy was not there.

Nailed to the wall was a page torn from *El Gráfico* with a photo of the Western Railway Soccer Team. On a newspaper spread out like a carpet over one of the trunks was an empty jar of hair gel, a comb, a toothbrush, and a pack of Barrilete cigarettes. The bed was unmade.

9

ANDREA ATTEMPTED TO ENLIST ME IN HER search for Miguel, but I managed to get free of her. I entered Mary's room in time to prevent the typist—that excessively busy incarnation of Muscarius, the god who shooed flies from altars—from committing an irreparable error. Indeed, she had already put the papers that were on the table in order, and was preparing to tidy the nightstand.

"Don't touch anything!" I shouted. "You are going to muddle the fingerprints."

I gave Cornejo and Atuel a severe look. The latter seemed to be smiling with veiled slyness.

My words did not ruffle the typist. She clutched the flyswatter. Her eyes took on a contented sibylline luster.

"I told you something was going to happen," she exclaimed. Then, whacking at the walls, she hurried off.

When the gong sounded Emilia said that she wasn't going upstairs to have lunch. With more impertinence than gallantry, Cornejo insisted on taking her place.

"I sympathize with you, Emilia. But believe me, the rest of us also feel responsible in the face of such a terrible tragedy. Your nerves are shattered. You should eat. We're all a little family here. As I am the eldest, I claim the honor of sitting with your sister."

A typical example of false courtesy: to inconvenience everyone in order to be kind to one person. Had he consulted me? And yet, he was putting me in the position of having to offer myself as a mourner and go without lunch. Furthermore, he himself had suggested that Emilia should feel responsible for her sister's death. It was only natural that she should want to spend a little time alone with her before the officials and the police arrived.

Atuel approached Emilia and spoke to her in a paternal tone:

"You should do whatever you want, Emilia." He caressed her arm. "If you would like lunch, I will stay, of course. If not, tell me if you want me to stay with you, or if you want to be alone. Do just as you like."

"The manner makes the man," I thought. Atuel's manner, like that of an overly debonair tango crooner, was beginning to exasperate me.

Emilia insisted on staying. I looked at her with the mixture of admiration and gratitude that men feel—sons of women, after all—toward the finest examples of the feminine spirit. As I was leaving, however, I noticed that in the midst of her pain Emilia had mustered the energy to change her clothes and powder her nose.

During lunch, the noise of the silverware and the drone of the flies were strangely pronounced. We spoke so little it made Manning seem almost chatty...

It is horrible to say it, but the members of our "little family" were eyeing one another with suspicion.

No one gave a thought to Miguel, except for Andrea. When we stood up, she took me aside.

"We haven't found him," she informed me. "Surely he's crying in the boat. Or in the sand. Or down in the crab bogs. We'll keep looking. When I have word, I'll let you know."

Why would she let *me* know? It irritated me that she would take me as an accomplice in these pseudo-maternal worries.

10

I FELT UNEXPECTEDLY CONTENT IN EMILIA'S company, and I venture to say that my presence didn't displease her.

There we were in that enormous rambling hotel, shut in as though it were a boat on the bottom of the ocean, or, more exactly, a foundered submarine. I felt that the air was becoming distressingly thin. I was uncomfortable everywhere, and I wouldn't be any more so in the dead girl's room. Besides, to accompany Emilia was an act of mercy.

Time itself acted strangely in that house. Some hours flew by, while others crept, and when I looked at my watch just before entering Mary's room, it was two in the afternoon. I would have guessed it was five o'clock.

We were alone in the room. Emilia asked me if I had known her sister well.

"No," I said. "Only in my capacity as a doctor. She visited my office two or three times." I added a kind lie: "I think she spoke of you on one occasion."

"We loved each other very much," Emilia commented. "Mary was so sweet to me... When my mother died, she took her place. Now she's left me alone."

"You have Atuel," I suggested, hypocritically.

Involuntarily, I had witnessed the incident of the night before: I had seen Mary kissing him.

"Poor man. It's affecting him almost as much as me," Emilia declared, and a noble splendor illuminated her face. "The three of us were very close."

A profound feeling of discomfort came over me.

"Are you two getting married soon?" I asked out of mere curiosity.

"I think so. But this has been so unexpected. . . For the time being I only want to think of Mary, to take refuge in my memories of our childhood in Tres Arroyos."

Experience has taught me that uncultured people, normally incapable of putting two words together, often utter poignant phrases when compelled by pain. I asked myself how well Humberto Huberman, with all his erudition, would acquit himself under similar circumstances.

"And now the police are coming," Emilia continued. "The worst part is that I don't even want to know the truth." Tears streamed down her face. "After what's happened I feel only a deep tenderness for Mary. I just can't resign myself to them tormenting her with the autopsy."

I thought this unreasonable, and I told her so quite frankly. "Sooner or later the decomposition process would do the same thing. But the truth matters to all of us, Emilia. Besides, Mary's memory lives on. No one can take that away."

The typist came in with a bouquet of wilting daisies. She laid it at the foot of the bed.

"They're the only flowers in the hotel," she said.

We watched her leave. Emilia might have murmured "thank you." We could no longer speak.

To break the silence, I asked, "Where were you last night, when you went out?"

"I was close by," she replied nervously. Hastily, she continued: "Leaning against one of the walls of the house. In that wind I couldn't go any farther. I came back right away. Andrea opened the door for me. The rest of you had already left."

The chairs creaked at our slightest movement. The physiological workings of our bodies took on a sudden preponderance. We sighed, we sneezed, we coughed.

For the first time in her life, Andrea arrived at an opportune moment. She appeared in the doorway and beckoned me.

Miguel had returned.

11

IN THE FLICKERING CANDLELIGHT, I WAS struck by Miguel's waxy complexion, intense gaze and rodent-like face. I registered a dizzy sensation that felt both unusual and unpleasant: I had lost my composure. Indeed, ensconced in the dim light of the trunk room, Miguel seemed determined to defend his mystery. My nervous imagination produced images of cornered animals, small and fierce.

The boy looked me straight in the eye. Instinctively, I avoided his obstinate expression and, feigning calm, I busied myself inspecting the trunks, the nightstand, the rickety cot, the walls. I lingered on the photograph of the soccer team; I had a brilliant idea.

"I see, my little friend, that you are also a Western Railway fan."

Not a flicker of simpatico illuminated Miguel's face.

"Have you ever been to the Quilmes Athletic Club?" I added. "Did you see the spot where Eliseo Brown's ball tore through the fence?"

Now Miguel smiled. Nevertheless, my knowledge of "the annals of soccer" had reached its limit. My next move in our dialogue would astutely combine the tactics of retreat and attack.

"Where did you spend the afternoon?" I asked casually. "You're not afraid of the storm?"

I remembered the abandoned sailboat, and thinking that we might speak in nautical terms, I consulted my memories of Conrad. Miguel answered abruptly:

"I went to Paulino Rocha's house."

"Who is Paulino Rocha?"

Miguel was surprised.

"The pharmacist," he explained.

I had regained my composure. I continued the interrogation.

"And what were you doing in the pharmacist's house?"

"I went to ask him to teach me how to preserve seaweed."

From beneath his cot, he pulled out a can of naphtha, with the rim crudely cut off. He tipped it toward me; some red and green strips floated in the liquid.

I now saw clearly into the soul of my small interlocutor. Little boys are the very incarnation of possibility. Miguel dabbled as a fisherman, a philatelist, a naturalist. A web of circumstances would determine—perhaps *I* would determine—if he would follow the easy meanderings of a collector or sportsman, or if he would venture out into the limitless avenues of science.

But I couldn't permit myself these musings, fertile and opportune though they may have been; I had to forge ahead, tirelessly, with my investigation.

"Did you love Mary a great deal?"

I understood as soon as I had formed the question

that I had made a mistake. Miguel looked intensely at the tin of naphtha, at the dark liquid, the seaweed. Once again he was defending his mystery.

It was too late to retreat. I tried to ascertain what the boy knew of the deceased's relationships, of Atuel and Emilia. My investigations in that direction got me nowhere. Likewise, his contribution to my knowledge of Esteban and Andrea was not particularly generous.

I lowered my eyes. Suddenly, I found myself staring at bloodstains on the floor. I moved two trunks slightly apart. A strangled cry rang out and I felt a sharp pain on my face—that boy's fingernails must have been poisoned; I still bear the scars. I was alone. On the floor, between the two trunks, was an enormous white bird, bathed in blood.

12

I HARBORED SERIOUS MISGIVINGS. I LOOKED outside, through the window in the grand hall. The storm had taken a turn for the worse.

My plan was precise: take tea; visit Emilia before the police arrived; receive the police. Yet I feared that my cousin's inexplicable delay in preparing, recipe in hand, some scones that aspired to equal Aunt Carlota's justifiably famous ones, might perhaps signal the downfall of this most reasonable plan. I looked out of the window again. I felt reassured. Waves of black water lashed the glass; the sand encroached. Then, in the brightness of the lightning flashes, I glimpsed an infernal landscape, the ground roiling and breaking apart, whipped into wrathful whirlwinds and waterspouts.

The dinner bell rang at last. The typist struck it in time to a gentle swaying of her head. Everyone, with the exception of Emilia, gathered in the dining room, around the tea tray. While I savored a judiciously golden scone, I thought of how the cardinal events—births, farewells, conspiracies, graduations, weddings, deaths—bring us together around pressed linen and timeless china; I remembered also that, for the Persians, a beautiful landscape served to stimulate the appetite and, expanding this idea, I decided that for the perfect man, all of life's vagaries should serve as stimuli.

In the deepest veins of thought, I heard the conversations around me merge with the buzzing of flies. It would not have surprised me—nor disturbed me—to hear the dry slap of the typist's (our friend Muscarius') swatter. Like one who reconstructs a jigsaw puzzle piece-by-piece, in putting those fragments of conversation together I discovered that there was, among us, a fearful cohort of people who, while masking their fear, secretly regretted having called the police, and who found hope in the wall of sand the storm was raising around the hotel.

I went downstairs to comfort Emilia.

I found her with her beautiful and placid face—the face of Dante's Proserpina came to mind—resting on her hand, clutching a lilac-colored handkerchief; the same posture in which I had left her hours earlier. Our conversation was insubstantial, though she did declare that Doctor Cornejo had insisted upon spending a few minutes alone with the body. Emilia had not allowed it.

I returned to the grand hall. Cornejo, seated rigidly on a modern chair and equipped with eyeglasses, paper and pencil, was studying an enormous tome. Whenever I come across someone reading, my first impulse is to snatch the book from his hands. I offer, for the curious, an exploration of this impulse: could it be an attraction to books, or impatience at finding myself displaced from the center of attention? I resigned myself to asking him what he was reading.

"A book of non-fiction," he replied. "A guide to loco-
motives. I carry in my mind a map of the country (limited to the railway lines, of course) in which I endeavor
to include even the most insignificant of locations, with
their respective distances and hours of departure..."

"You are interested in the fourth dimension, the
space-time continuum," I declared.

"The literature of evasion, I'd call it," Manning observed, enigmatically.

Atuel was looking out the window. He called us over.
Engulfed in a furious cyclone of sand, we saw the Rickenbacker. For the first time all day, I laughed. I confess:
the absurdity of the scene unfolding with cinematic
diligence was quite compelling. Out of the car emerged
one, two, three, four, six people in all. They huddled
against one of the car's rear doors. Laboriously, they extracted a large, darkly colored object. I watched them—
my eyes tearing with laughter—as they approached the
hotel, tripping blindly in the sand, as though it were
the dark of night, struggling and knocking about in the
wind, their forms misshapen by the oblique effect of
the windowpane. They were bringing the coffin.

13

WE GREETED COMMISSIONER RAIMUNDO
Aubry and Doctor Cecilio Montes, the police physician, with a glass of bitters, cheese sandwiches, and
olives. Meanwhile, Esteban, the chauffeur, two police
officers and a man wearing a light-colored suit and a
black armband—"the Master of Ceremonies," as I was
told—carried the coffin down to the basement.

Right away I began to regret the glass of bitters that
I myself had served to Doctor Montes. I had not yet
discovered that one more drink could never have much
altered my young colleague's state. The doctor was
drunk; he had arrived drunk.

Cecilio Montes was a man of medium height and
fragile build. He had dark wavy hair, large eyes, extremely pale skin, a finely boned face and a straight
nose. He was dressed in a greenish cheviot hunting-
suit, quite well cut, that, once upon a time, had been of
high quality. His silk shirt was dirty. The hallmarks of
his general aspect were slovenliness, neglect, ruin—a
ruin that yet allowed glimpses of a former glory. I asked
myself how this character, an escapee from a Russian
novel, had appeared in our midst; I discovered unexpected analogies between the Argentine and Russian

landscapes, and between the souls of our respective peoples: I imagined the young doctor arriving in Salinas, his faith in noble causes and in civilization, and his gradual deterioration, faced with the hardships and small-mindedness intrinsic to small town life. *J'avais calé mon Oblomov*. I regarded him with utmost sympathy.

For his part, however, he appeared to lack even that most minimal and rudimentary sympathy that, out of loneliness, indomitably draws together members of the same guild or profession. He scarcely answered my questions, and when he did answer them, his manner vacillated between indifference and aggression. I did manage to remind myself that Montes was drunk, and that, on earlier occasions, when that same spontaneous sympathy had impelled me toward my colleagues, I had been met only with souls withered by the superstitions of nineteenth-century scientific positivism.

Commissioner Aubry was a tall man, ruddy, with suntanned skin and an expression of perpetual astonishment in his light blue eyes. I wish to pause a moment on those eyes, because they were the man's most distinctive feature. They were not excessively large, nor were they, as one might say, magnetic, sharp, or penetrating; but it must be said that the Commissioner's entire life vibrated from within them, and that he listened and thought through them. One would scarcely have begun speaking to him and, immediately, the Commissioner's eyes would fix upon his interlocutor with such intensity and expectation that the speaker's ideas would become muddled and his words devolve into hopeless stammering.

"Have no doubt; this is a case of strychnine poisoning," I affirmed gravely.

"We shall see, my esteemed colleague, we shall see," said Montes. He turned his back to me and addressed the Commissioner.

"Make a note: a suspicious attempt to impose a diagnosis."

"My dear sir," I replied, involuntarily choosing a term of address as false as the situation. "Were you not inebriated, you would never permit yourself such fatuous words."

"Some people do not need to be drunk to speak fatuously," Montes replied.

I was readying myself to formulate a retort that would obliterate that dipsomaniac, when the Commissioner intervened.

"Gentlemen," he said, seeking me out with those inexorable eyes. "Might you show us to the deceased's room?"

With perfect composure, I led them downstairs. When we arrived at Mary's door, I opened it and stood aside so that the Commissioner could enter. Doctor Montes entered as well, brandishing his little cloth medicine kit. Perhaps due to the associations that medicine kit evoked, I murmured:

"Mary's soul is no longer in need of a midwife."

14

CONTRARY TO HIS MOST DEARLY HELD HOPES, Doctor Montes was forced to agree with my diagnosis. Mary had died from strychnine poisoning.

Calmly and authoritatively, the Commissioner ordered the police officers to follow him.

"With your permission," he told us, " we shall move on to a search of each of your rooms."

I approved the course of action. The Commissioner addressed me:

"We'll begin with yours, Doctor. Unless anyone present cares to declare possession of strychnine."

No one responded. Not even I. The Commissioner's words had stunned me. I had never imagined that they would search *my* room.

"Do not involve me in this matter," I said at last. "I am a doctor. . . I demand to be respected."

"Forgive me," replied the Commissioner. "Everyone must be measured by the same yardstick."

He seemed to be suggesting that this "stick" was not merely metaphorical.

Reluctantly I led, or, more accurately, followed them to my room. My very own Mount Calvary awaited me, along with the satisfaction of confirming the perfect control I maintain over my nerves. Helpless, as if they had injected me with curare, I was obliged to stand tolerantly by as those rude hands defiled the interior of my suitcase and, even more stupefying, as, one by one, they opened the vials in my medicine kit, fragile and delicate as virgins.

"Be careful, gentlemen!" I exclaimed, unable to contain myself. "Those are extremely precise dosages. Don't you understand? Any odor, any contact at all can negate the efficacy of those medications."

I had achieved my goal. The men set upon my medicine kit with renewed ferocity. I slipped between the violators and the nightstand. With my right hand resting casually on the marble tabletop, I retrieved the vial of arsenic. I was prepared to suffer any indignity save the confiscation of those drops, the pillars of my health.

When the police at last finished their inspection of my medicine kit, I dropped the arsenic in among the other vials. I believed myself saved, but fate had reserved other trials for me. Sending a chill through my very soul, I heard the Commissioner declare:

"Next we'll have a look at the pills."

I decoded his ignorant words: he was referring to my drops. Naturally, I assumed he would inspect them right then and there. But Commissioner Aubry, with a lack of logic equaled only by his lack of courtesy, moved on to Cornejo's room, leaving me free to take whatever precautions I deemed prudent.

15

I WON'T HESITATE TO MENTION THAT THE others' rooms did not garner the same prolonged, minute examination that Commissioner Aubry had designated for the room of Doctor Humberto Huberman.

I did not stand idly by while the police entourage continued its inspection of the hotel. After putting my room back in order, I began my own investigation... I went out into the hallway. How surprised I was to discover that not a single officer was guarding the scene of the crime! I stationed myself in the shadows, in the very same spot from which Miguel had eavesdropped on the arguments between Emilia and Mary. Immediately, I remembered that I had surprised Miguel there and, with a sudden terror, realized that I, too, might be so surprised.

I was about to flee, when the sound of footsteps detained me. It was the typist. I was beginning to recognize, one by one, the elements of that hermetic hotel, of that limited world (as the prisoner recognizes the jailhouse rats and the patient the design of the hospital's wallpaper or the molding on the ceiling). Brandishing her swatter, the huntress appeared in the dim light. She wheeled about dangerously, following the trajectory of the flies. Then she disappeared into the darkness of the corridors.

I waited a bit longer. It didn't matter that the typist had surprised me; it would be best, however, for no one to discover that I had been hiding outside Mary's room. I waited too long. Atuel came slowly down the stairs. He approached with a mixture of caution and determination that paralyzed me, and I had the sudden realization that a man I had, until that moment, regarded with indifference, had criminal potential. He entered Mary's room. He pulled a suitcase from under the bed. He opened it and rummaged through it. Then he looked through the papers on the table. He appeared to be looking for something. His extraordinary composure seemed unnatural; I was put in mind of a talented actor who knows he has an audience, but disregards it... Pearls of cold sweat stood out on my forehead. Atuel set the papers aside; he took a red book from the nightstand (I recognized the book: it was a novel in English, with an emblem of superimposed masks and pistols on the cover); he put the book in his pocket; he walked to the door; he looked this way and that; he took several long, silent steps; he stopped again; I saw him ascend the stairs, taking them four at a time.

I left at last. If I stayed any longer, the police would discover me. I instructed my cousin to prepare me some white toast.

16

THE COMMISSIONER CALLED US TOGETHER in the dining room.

"Gentlemen," he said, with stentorian gravity. "I hope that you are all prepared to testify. I will set myself up in the manager's office and you will come to me, one by one, like sheep at a watering hole."

"Don't you have a sense of humor? Why aren't you laughing?" Montes asked me.

I was about to issue a pointed response, but the smell of alcohol on his breath caused me to retreat.

The interrogations began. I was among the first to be called in. Although they didn't pressure me, I told them all that I knew, not omitting a single detail that might help guide the investigation. Like a benevolent crime novelist, I restricted myself to dispensing appropriate emphasis. I was confident that, under my yoke, even Aubry's modest intelligence would succeed in solving the mystery.

As I was leaving the office, I became aware that a crucial omission had tarnished my exposition. I tried to go back in, but they would not admit me. I would be forced to wait until all the other witnesses had offered up their longwinded babblings. Purgatory is never brief.

It would not, perhaps, be futile, to recount here one small detail—which Aubry shared with me in subsequent conversations—from Andrea's testimony. It seems that the night before, my cousin, as was her habit, had placed a cup of hot chocolate on Mary's bedside table. Now the cup was gone. Andrea admitted that she hadn't noticed its absence at first, and offered, by means of an explanation, the delicate condition of her nerves.

The white toast I had ordered arrived at last. My spirit was revived.

When they summoned me, I did not jump up as one receiving an order, but rather rose, as one seeking recompense. As I entered the office I whispered the time-honored verse:

At last, a bird passed by.
Out of the mist he did fly.
With a wave of my hand, I greeted him
As though he were a good Christian.

I looked at the Commissioner in silence. Then, I announced dramatically:

"In a boy's room, in the basement of this hotel, hidden among some trunks, there is a dead bird. An albatross. I found it this afternoon, with its chest torn open, its entrails gone." I paused, then continued. "Just a few hours later, while Doctor Montes was examining the body of the dead girl, in the basement, a pair of solitary hands was embalming the albatross. What are we to make of these symmetrical events? The poison that kills the girl, in the bird, preserves the simulacrum of life."

17

MY REVELATION BORE ITS FIRST FRUIT THAT very night. Effortlessly, with the silent naturalness of the necessary, I shifted from the group of suspects to the group of investigators. In fact, in a private parley, Commissioner Aubry, Doctor Montes and I lingered over coffee and sour cherries until the sun began to come up over the sand dunes.

My colleague wanted to discuss women; the Commissioner elevated our spirits discussing books. He was a devotee of *Count Kostia*, tolerated *Fabiola* and disapproved of *Ben-Hur*, but his favorite book was *The Man Who Laughs*. His blue eyes regarded me with intense solemnity.

"Do you not find," he asked me, "that the most important moment in literature is when Victor Hugo describes that English lord, an aficionado of cockfights, who dances at a club with two women on his arm? He offers a dowry to the single one and makes the other's husband Chaplain."

I was pleasantly taken aback by Aubry's literary fervor, and uncomfortably perplexed by his question. By a generous twist of fate, the sentence that allowed me to evade giving an answer was also a useful piece of advice. I recommended that he read a few modern works: in particular, Thomas Mann's *The Magic Mountain*, a novel pertinent to our circumstances and of which not a single copy was to be found in the hotel.

He listened to me eagerly, even reverently. It was as though his light-blue eyes were fixed upon my words. Perhaps they fixed them in his memory. My lips were still uttering the words "Thomas Mann," when, laboriously, as one toiling "through the dark reaches of obscurity" in search of a few verses, he said:

"Hardquanonne says: 'There exists an honesty in hell.'" Phrases such as these reveal the great listener; they set the true genius apart.

My entire life has been marked by such encounters with would-be friends: so long as they think in the abstract, we understand one another; they give a specific example, and incompatibility rears its head. With a warm burst of sympathy, the authenticity of which we need not examine, we continued speaking of literature until Doctor Montes interrupted his sullen silence in order to ask:

"What conclusions have been reached in the investigation?"

His eyes, arched and alert, fixed first on Aubry, then on me; his mouth, moving like a ruminant's, savored a sour cherry. Already prepared to admonish myself for any lack of courtesy, I asked myself how far I had advanced in the man's confidence. I did not possess unlimited faith in Aubry's explanation of the mystery. Nevertheless, I was eager to learn what it might be.

18

"I KNEW FROM THE BEGINNING WHO THE guilty party was," the Commissioner asserted, leaning forward in a gesture of confidentiality and squinting at us as though looking into the horizon. "The subsequent investigation and interrogations only confirmed my suspicion."

I felt inclined to believe him. Complicated crimes were the province of literature; reality was more banal (I was reminded of Petronius and his pirates, standing in chains on the beach). Furthermore, presumably Aubry possessed some experience in the subject matter. In novels (to return, for a moment, to literature) police officials are infallibly mistaken. In reality, they are something far worse, yet they tend not to fail, because crime, like madness, is a product of simplification and deficiency.

"Gentlemen," said Doctor Montes, mystifyingly. "Will you allow me to make a toast?"

"In honor of what?" asked the Commissioner.

"Of the marvelous truths we are about to hear."

I was secretly pleased by his response. What could one really hope for from an investigator who paid heed to the blathering of a drunk?

The Commissioner continued:

"We'll begin with the motives. To our knowledge, there are two people with enduring motives to commit the crime."

"In saying 'to our knowledge,'" interrupted the drunk, with more logic than tact, "you acknowledge that there are things we do not know, and, as such, your explanation falls apart."

"As I was saying, in terms of motive, there are two people who merit our particular attention," continued the Commissioner, as if he had not even registered Montes's impertinence. "The victim's sister and Mr. Atuel."

I was dismayed. I must confess, from that moment on, I had to struggle to follow Aubry's explanations. My imagination wandered through a sort of cinematic spectacle; the scenes occurred in reverse order—first, my last conversations with Emilia; finally, the episode on the beach—and my interpretation of the events had changed as well; now, upon reviewing the arguments between the sisters, Emilia was the good girl. I thought of Mary and I told myself that a person's actions have a trajectory, with changes and fluctuations, that extends beyond death. I thought of Emilia and I asked myself if, perhaps, I had begun to love her.

Aubry's "explanation" had a touch of technical braggadocio about it; I will try to repeat it, in his words.

"Let us say that motives are classified as either enduring or fleeting," he said, his expression stern. "In the present case, the primary motives involve questions of economics and of passion. This death benefits Miss Emilia Gutiérrez and Mr. Atuel. Miss Emilia is her sister's heir. She will receive some pieces of jewelry that are, and I do not believe I exaggerate, quite valuable. And, as I learned through the interrogations, the fiancés had postponed their wedding because of economic difficulties. As for Mr. Atuel, he, too, will benefit from the death, through marriage. The motive of passion points to the same two people. It seems to be a well-known fact that the deceased was romantically involved with Miss Emilia's fiancé. And so, we have jealousy, the catalyst for the tragedy. Unfortunately for Emilia, this is a purely feminine feature. But the entanglement between the fiancé and the victim must be considered a hotbed of violent passions, which also points to the first of the suspects. Moving on to the fleeting motives. The last quarrels occurred between the sisters, and largely excluded the fiancé—also unfortunate for Miss Emilia! Finally, let us move from the motives to the occasion. This is the point in our investigation where Atuel is ruled out: he was not in the hotel at the time of the death. He is residing in the New East End Hotel. The two sisters were staying in adjoining rooms. As you will all remember, on the night of the tragedy, Miss Emilia went down to their rooms alone. There she put the strychnine in the hot chocolate; waited for the poison to work; made the cup disappear (perhaps she threw it out a window; when the storm passes we will sift through the sand). Conclusion: unless the devil steps in to help her, is there any way out for the young lady?"

I suspected that there were imperfections in the logical structure of those arguments, but I was too confused and heavy-hearted to ferret them out. I managed to protest:

"Your explanation is psychologically impossible. You remind me of one of those novelists who focuses entirely on action but neglects the characters. Do not forget that, without the human element, no work of literature would ever endure. Have you thought closely about Emilia? I refuse to accept that such a healthy girl (albeit, a bit redheaded) could have committed this crime."

I had gone a bit too far in trying to replace a logical argument with a mere emotional improvisation. The Commissioner said:

"I shall allow Victor Hugo to respond to you: 'Agony makes a vice of a woman's fingers. A girl in her fright can almost bury her rose-colored fingers in a piece of iron.'"

Doctor Montes appeared to awake from his lethargy.

"If I were not so drunk, I would tell you that your entire case is based upon presumptions," he explained affectionately to the Commissioner. "You do not have a single shred of evidence."

"That does not bother me," replied Aubry. "I will have all the proof you want when we make her talk down at the station."

I looked uncomprehendingly at that man who reasoned crudely but efficiently, who was ardently fond of literature, who was moved by Hugo, and who, without hesitation, was prepared to torture a young girl and to condemn her, perhaps unjustly.

I was surprised to find myself looking sympathetically at Montes. There had been much to forgive in him, but perhaps, as two doctors, together, we would make one good attorney.

And what was I to make of Emilia's mysterious power? I, an essentially vindictive sort, felt inclined, on her behalf, to fraternize with a colleague who had earlier insulted me. At that very moment, I hit upon the answer to a question I had posed to myself a short while before. It was not love I was feeling: it was an ambiguous feeling of guilt. I was, in that limited world of Bosque del Mar, the dominant intellect, and my statements had guided the investigation. To reassure myself that I had only carried out my duty was insufficient, even as a consolation.

"An obvious tactic," offered Montes, "would be to link the poison to someone; to verify, for example, who has bought strychnine at the pharmacy..."

"I have not overlooked that measure," responded Aubry authoritatively. "I sent one of my officers with precise instructions: ask the pharmacist to whom he has sold strychnine in the last few months. The answer was categorical: to no one."

With feigned casualness, I asked: "What is your plan, Commissioner?"

"My plan? To say not a word to the girl until the storm has passed. Then I'll arrest her and take her in. I ask you all to remain calm. She will not be able to flee. Nor will she be able to destroy the evidence since, as you know, it is contained in the interrogations. Our mission, for the time being, is to remain quiet; wait for the storm to pass."

I got up impatiently. I looked out the window. A drab, sandy dawn was filtering through the gale. The world outside looked like the ruins of a yellow fire. Spirals of sand, like frenzied smoke, whipped up from the dark shapes of fallen posts. Nevertheless, I asked myself whether, in fact, the storm was continuing with the same intensity, and with fear in my heart I searched for signs of impending calm.

I rested one hand, then the other, then my forehead, upon the glass. It felt cool to the touch, as though I had a fever.

19

DREAMS ARE OUR DAILY PRACTICE OF MADNESS. At the moment we go truly insane we say to ourselves: "This world is familiar to me. I have visited it nearly every night of my life." Thus, when we believe that we are dreaming but are, in fact, awake, our sense of reason tilts into vertigo.

I heard Liszt's *Forgotten Waltz* issuing from a piano, the same waltz Emilia had played the night before. Were we still locked up in that hotel, in the middle of a sandstorm, with the dead girl in her room? Or, inexplicably, had I lost myself and begun retracing my steps backwards in time? I awoke that morning with the blind, choking, anguished need to escape that some patients experience in the fog of anesthesia. I could not open the window, but in a fit of hope I decided to leave the room. I opened the door: no relief, the same heaviness and inescapable sound of the *Forgotten Waltz*.

I climbed the stairs slowly. Now, as if waking from a dream, I was startled by reality, yet the music persisted like a relic of insanity. I went to seek its source, wary of its disappearance, already feeling nostalgic for the miracle of it.

I entered the dining room. Manning was playing

solitaire next to the radio, from which issued the *Forgotten Waltz*.

"Do you not find this music inappropriate under the circumstances?" I asked him.

He looked at me as if he were just waking up.

"Music?... Forgive me... I wasn't listening to it. I turned on the radio to hear the news. Then I started playing and forgot all about it."

I switched the radio off.

"You are the king of solitaire," I told him.

"Don't believe it," he replied. "A friend once told me that out of every thousand hands one will win seventy-five. I thought he was exaggerating."

"And so, you are testing the theory?"

I realized that, with Manning, I was employing an uncharacteristically protective tone. He was so unusually small.

While he attempted to explain something about the calculation of probabilities, I moved closer to the window. It seemed impossible that there were sunny skies somewhere out there beyond our opaque one. I felt disgusted by those interminable sandy winds.

A spider sat in a corner of the window.

"They are bad luck at this hour of the day," I declared. I seized a newspaper with which to squash it.

"Don't kill it," begged Manning. "It came out of the radio because of the music. I put it in that corner two or three days ago and just look at the web it has made."

I looked. I saw a tangle of filthy threads and a dried-up fly.

"Huberman," a voice boomed. "We need you."

It was Cornejo. He was dressed in white flannel pants and a sport shirt. Something in his voice reminded me of a ship's captain, issuing his final orders as the ship went down.

"Come to the office," he continued. "They are going to seal the coffin. You should accompany Emilia."

It is always a comfort to encounter individuals capable of valuing my qualities as a spiritual guide.

In the office, Atuel, Montes, and the Commissioner were with Emilia.

"I'm going downstairs," declared Cornejo, and he departed, with perfect composure.

With a warm feeling of responsibility, I tried to approach Emilia. Atuel and Montes were talking with her. While I debated with the Commissioner about our prospects with the weather, I observed them; the men, at ease, indistinct; Emilia, uncomfortable in her chair, rigid, with that air of an actor on stage often displayed by those in pain. Suddenly, I wondered if Cornejo had brought me to the office because Emilia needed me, or because *he* needed me not to be elsewhere.

A nearby clanging of dishes and silverware announced the proximity of breakfast. I had no choice but to discard these disagreeable thoughts. Indeed, in the daily ceremony of the first meal, I see the characteristics of emotional poetry that are reborn through repetition, inviolable and pristine. I took the vial of arsenic from my pocket and deposited the requisite ten drops into the palm of my left hand. As I raised them to my mouth, I glimpsed a flash of surprise in Commissioner Aubry's honest eyes. I blushed like a child.

Cornejo appeared in the doorway. He was pale, terrifyingly pale, as though a sudden old age had overcome him. He leaned heavily on the table.

"I must speak with you, Commissioner," he said in a tired voice.

The Commissioner and I went over to him. Atuel appeared engrossed in the impenetrable view through the window. Emilia left, followed imprudently by Montes.

20

IN THE PAINTING BY ALONSO CANO, DEATH
places a frozen kiss on the lips of a sleeping boy.

After leaving the office, Cornejo had gone in the
direction of Mary's room. He wanted someone, aside
from the undertaker and some predictable policeman,
to bid farewell to the dead girl at the moment of seal-
ing her coffin. On his way, he met up with the undertaker who told him that he was going downstairs to
look for some tools. Going along the hallway, Cornejo
tore three pages off the "Lobster" espadrilles calendar
to bring it up to date (I carefully list these details as if
they were important to the story, or perhaps to the narrator, or simply to keep him from getting distracted, as
in the case of the plans he had traced the other night
on the tablecloth). Then he went into Mary's room. At
this point Cornejo fell suddenly silent, shuddered, and
wiped his forehead with a handkerchief. We thought
he was going to faint. What he had witnessed was atro-
cious: a rush of intensity comes over us when we first
recount the experiences we have by ourselves. What
Cornejo saw (he assured us) was so horrible that ever
since that moment, the mere image of the door to
that room, in his memories and his dreams, would be

utterly terrifying. In the lonely center of that room, in the heart of the silence and utter stillness of that house buried in the sand, he saw—in the wavering candlelight that seemed to project the shadows of some invisible foliage—Miguel, a mere child, kiss the lips of the dead girl.

"When he saw you, what did the boy do?"

"He ran away," Cornejo replied, after a pause.

"Who remained in the room with the dead girl?"

"When I left, the typist entered. That boy has to be questioned immediately."

"Doesn't seem wise to me," Aubry observed. "We'll get into trouble with his aunt."

I agreed.

"Children are very impressionable," I said. "He might be traumatized by us, scarred for life."

Doctor Cornejo looked at me as if he didn't understand Spanish.

"If we speak to him so soon after the event," the Police Chief remarked, "we'd be forcing him to lie. And you know very well that one fib leads to another..."

I was about to say something, but the Commissioner stopped me.

"Don't say a word," he begged me. "Don't add anything to what you've said. What you've already said is perfect. It reminds me of Hugo's words about harsh experiences when they happen too early in life, that they construct in the souls of children a formidable sort of scale upon which they weigh God."

21

DOUBTLESSLY, IN THE COMMISSIONER'S mind, Emilia was still a key suspect. The others were thinking only of Miguel, or perhaps of Miguel and Cornejo. It seemed that the rest of us were excluded from the drama.

I felt an urgency to talk, to communicate what Aubry had confided in me. I knew that Emilia was in danger of being detained and even of being tortured. I believed in her innocence. I was convinced that a tactical defensive move was required. If we didn't take immediate advantage of what I knew, later on it would be too late to defend her. I was overwhelmed by the responsibility.

I was held back by a grave uncertainty. At first I had thought of speaking with Emilia. In general I get along better with women than with men (of course Emilia was a young woman and the company I prefer is that of mature women). On the other hand, my news could frighten her. I took into consideration that it wasn't prudent to tell secrets that could harm me to a person agitated by fear. I decided to speak to Atuel—a conversation that would be less pleasant, but favored by such merits as security and sanity, so reassuring to those of us whose lives are buttressed by an austere sense of balance. I concluded that Atuel's links with Emilia would preclude any future risk for me.

I looked for him in Mary's room, then in Emilia's, in

the dining room, the office, the basement. I methodically checked every room in the hotel. Aubry told me he hadn't seen him; Andrea looked at me suspiciously; Montes threw me out of his room and threatened me with a lawsuit for trespassing; the typist, as if distracted and in a rush, answered:

"He's in Doctor Manning's room."

I found them lounging in armchairs, unforgivably submerged in the most inconceivable frivolity. Manning was reading the English novel that Atuel had stolen from Mary's room. Atuel was reading one of those novels with a ridiculous harlequin cover, which Mary had translated. On a table placed between the readers were papers scribbled with notes, and pencils. They were taking notes on detective novels!

If Atuel was stooping to such childish activities, he must have been unaware of the Commissioner's intentions. I was convinced that I had to warn him immediately. I thought, not without satisfaction, of the regret the poor man would feel when he found out about the danger his fiancée was in.

I must admit that surprising deceptions still awaited me, whose traces—now erased, of course—would not form scar tissue as quickly as I desired. When I declared: "I have something important to tell you," Atuel's interest in hearing what I had to say seemed less evident than his annoyance at the interruption of his unseemly reading. Without omitting any detail I reported the news to him. He listened to me with visible deference, thanked me, and, incredibly, returned immediately to his novel.

22

COMMISSIONER AUBRY GRABBED THE
enormous embalmed albatross.

Tied to the neck of the bird with a green ribbon
hung a little boy's photograph, with the inscription, *To
My Dear Parents, a souvenir from Miguel.* In the whiteness of its breast I saw all the nostalgia of the days in
which the light, "shadow of the gods," illuminates with
limpid clarity the world beside the sea, days that, for us,
seemed definitively buried under the sandstorm.

In the trunk itself, wrapped in newspaper, we found
a small amount of arsenic. For the past twenty minutes,
Commissioner Aubry, Andrea and I had been searching Miguel's room. The Commissioner asked Andrea:

"Do you think that Miguel was able to embalm the
bird all by himself?"

"I think so," the woman answered. "He spends his
whole life. . ."

"What reasons would he have had to hide it?" Aubry
interrupted.

"He knew I didn't like it. While he was in the house,
he couldn't torture animals. We had forbidden it. I believe that cruelty in children should be repressed."

Aubry showed her the packet of arsenic.

"Did you know that the boy had this poison?"

Andrea didn't know, nor did she know that the poison was used in taxidermy and in the preservation of algae.

The Commissioner told her she could go. We remained alone, considering the possible connections between our findings and Mary's death. But in the cause-and-effect account we tried to establish, there was a fatal gap. The poison that killed Mary wasn't arsenic.

It was necessary for Doctor Cornejo to witness the boy's horrific kiss in order for Aubry to take into account my accusation with reference to the embalmed bird. From that moment on I was given the consideration I deserved. Aubry consulted me for everything. Perhaps one could object to this manner of conducting an investigation. Why didn't Aubry look for fingerprints? Why didn't he order an autopsy of the corpse? Only a small-town detective—one might add—would take on a stranger as his confidant. But it's not difficult to respond to these objections. With fingerprints he wouldn't make much progress (all our fingerprints, without any doubt, would show up); the autopsy would prove what everyone already knew (that she had been poisoned by strychnine); after all, I am not a stranger, and this way of proceeding as if we were all a family has its advantages: it creates an atmosphere of trust, in which the suspect will inadvertently forget to be cautious.

With ridiculous timidity Manning knocked on the

door. He had something important—he dared to pronounce the word "important"—to declare. With pleasure I heard this reply from the Commissioner:

"I beseech you to postpone your revelation until after tea."

23

EVERYONE LEFT THE DINING ROOM AFTER tea, except for Atuel, Aubry, Montes and myself.

"Let's see what Doctor Manning here has to tell us."

"I have already discussed the hypothesis I am going to propose with Inspector Atwell."

First I thought I had heard wrong, but then, by virtue of that sentence the world was transformed, and what was familiar became unknown and dangerous. I barely contained my irritation:

I repeated: "Atuel, Atwell." Manning explained: "I don't deserve credit. It was just luck. As you folks know, yesterday morning I spent a long time in Miss Mary's room. The table was covered with papers. Suddenly, on a notepad page I read a phrase that drew my attention. Perhaps I gave it excessive importance: I copied it. When we went up to the dining room I told Atwell about it."

Commissioner Aubry put out the cigarette he had just lit in the ashtray and said:

"I'm not in the mood, Inspector, to reprimand you, but why didn't you say anything? As soon as I knew who you were, I asked for your collaboration."

"How could I bother you with a suggestion I myself

didn't believe? But let's not be hindered by matters of procedure: the important thing is results. Let Manning tell us."

"You folks probably didn't see the piece of paper because the typist tidied up the table," the doctor explained. "There were galley proofs and handwritten pages, the latter being the translation Miss Gutiérrez was doing of a novel by Michael Innes. As it was part of a continuous text, you folks did not keep reading, but the page should be there."

The Commissioner breathed with a heavy sigh. His frustration was visible. Manning continued:

"The phrase in question was either part of a book or a message from Miss Gutiérrez. The former could be easily determined. The night before her death, the young lady told us that she had in her room a small library made up of all the novels she had translated. I asked the Commissioner to let me read the handwritten pages. He told me we couldn't touch them. I got him to let me read the books: they were less personal objects. On these last two evenings I have read the original of the novel the young lady was translating and a good part of the books already translated. The Inspector read the rest. We have worked conscientiously. We can assure you that the phrase does not figure in any of the books."

There was a silence. Finally the Commissioner exclaimed:

"Dear Inspector, what a way to collaborate with your colleagues!"

In the tone of these words I thought I detected that Aubry was resentful, accepted Manning's solution and had no curiosity to hear it. As far as I was concerned, I couldn't suppress my curiosity (I pride myself on it: our hold on life is measured by the intensity of our passions). I begged Manning not to delay any longer in communicating the phrase, the key that permitted him and Atwell to penetrate a mystery that still remained obscure to the rest of us.

"What Miss Gutiérrez wrote before dying is this," Manning replied monotonously. Then he read from a piece of paper:

Sorrowfully I must announce to you my decision, which I know too well will leave you in a state of shock, and if something in this hard world could induce me to abandon my resolve it would be our long friendship and the thought of your good will and your affection. But things have reached such a point that the only thing I can possibly do is to say farewell to the world and leave it.

24

AS WRITERS WHO FOLLOW THE CALL OF THE vocation and not the pursuit of wealth, our fate is a continuous search for pretexts to postpone the moment of putting the pen to paper. How solicitously doth reality provide those pretexts and with what delicate devotion does it conspire with our indolence! I could not continue to be bewitched by that sterile problem of suicide, or murder, in Bosque del Mar. The time to react had arrived. I withdrew into the silence and asylum of my room, sank into the comfortable embrace of the armchair, opened the almost virginal notebook and the book by Petronius. I thought of Mary.

As one investigating a text capable of subtly contradictory interpretations, I re-examined the dispute between the two sisters that happened the night before Mary's death. I also probed the motives that could lead a suicide to leave her posthumous message lost among papers.

I wondered if this last act were not one of tortuous honesty. Through it Mary placated her conscience. She left the proof that would save an innocent person, but she left it hidden.

This suicide was the inevitable end of a drama of

which I had caught a glimpse. With the desperate ve-
hemence of bad causes, Mary falls in love with Emilia's
fiancé. Secretly she tries to take him away from her.
When she sees that she's losing, she resolves to die. In
the project of her death she finds the sweetness of re-
venge. And if someone were to interpret the suicide as
murder? On her last night she manages to make Emilia
angry with her. Then she writes the message declaring
that she dies by her own hand, but writes it on a sheet
of paper identical to those she uses for her translation
of Michael Innes; she places it among the translation
papers. She lets it be discovered and revealed by chance
and thus believes she will save her soul.

I next considered Atwell's role in the investigation.
He told me that he hadn't wanted to intrude upon the
procedures because of something I didn't understand
about the general rules of the law and because of his
relationship with Emilia and with Mary. The argument
seemed convincing to me. I'm a doctor and I know how
feelings get in the way of our professional judgment.
He added, besides, that he hadn't wanted to offend the
emotional susceptibility of the Commissioner.

I did not resign myself to admitting that Atwell's
participation was as simple as he would like it to seem.
It seemed obvious that Manning had succeeded in solving the mystery. But had he done it alone? In Manning's
deductions, couldn't one divine the directing mind of
Atwell?

Later, I took Aubry aside and asked him who the
Inspector was.

"The most valuable man of the lot," he answered. "Atwell is so famous today that to take time off he has to go incognito like a king."

I looked into Aubry's eyes. They did not express any irony. They expressed respect.

"The lot" was the police department of the Federal Capital. Atwell worked in the Investigative Analysis Division.

25

AFTER DINNER THERE WAS A MOMENT IN which Emilia and I were sitting alone at one end of the table. I took immediate advantage of it. "I have to talk to you," I said with an emphasis that in my attempt not to seem amatory came out heavy-handed. I suspect that she didn't then know what I had to talk to her about. But I had to talk because I felt in me that social, gregarious instinct that is one of the most noble and beneficial traits of the human spirit.

Nobody was watching us. I took Emilia's hand and, with a feeling that came from the bottom of my heart, I communicated to her the Commissioner's sinister conjectures. She didn't take her hand away. Nor did she answer me. No amazement, no disappointment seemed to perturb her serene grief. I should have been glad, but inexplicably I felt cheated.

Very soon, however, I was grateful to realize that I owed the recovery of my good sense to Emilia's apparent coolness. How I had dramatized my sympathy and concern for the girl! What a relief to find myself free of that unjustifiable madness!

It's difficult to acknowledge, but the mystery of Mary's death was beginning to wear down the perfect equilibrium of my nerves. I decided to go to bed early to

regain my strength. I said "Good night" and went to the
office to fill my pen with ink and leave it ready for the
literary labors of the next morning. When I entered the
room, Atwell and the Commissioner were examining a
piece of paper. They handed it to me. It had neither a
heading nor a date nor a signature. It was Mary's message. What suffering, what unhealthy intentions were
betrayed by the complicated and bombastic features of
that handwriting to those of us who never turned our
backs on the truths of graphology! But now it is time to
probe the occult sciences, to reread and write again the
muddle of books composed with the criteria, methods,
and ink of the darkest Middle Ages, to undertake the
Great Adventure, the voyages, without a compass, of
the astrologer, the alchemist and the magician. Men
of every profession awaken today to the Marvelous
Dream... But, who will deny that it is among the ho-
meopaths that we recruit the most vigorous champions
of the new crusade?

The Commissioner looked with his austere eyes at
the Inspector and gravely pronounced:

"With all due respect, I still think that the suppositions against Miss Emilia are conclusive. My plans
have not changed: to arrest her and take her to Salinas.
They will be carried out unless the matter passes into
the hands of others."

Instinctively I tried to looked outside but in the
white wall the window was a rectangle as dark and impenetrable as onyx. I pressed my ear against the glass. It
seemed that the wind was dying down.

26

I REMEMBERED, LIKE SOMETHING UNREACHABLE, those mornings in my home in the city, which began with the provincial servants bringing the wicker tray, the fragrant tea, the toast and the pastries, the jam and the honey. That was indeed a "happy awakening," as they say in the primary-school books; then came the pleasures of leisure, books, and then the chance events of the afternoon, the office with rewards for the professional and for the man. My real vacation had remained back there, with those domestic and everyday rituals that now seemed lost. What anxieties would the new day bring? Fearful, skeptical about my fear (it seemed incredible that this abnormality was continuing to upset my life), I opened the door to my room. Upon reaching the staircase I met up with Andrea.

"Did you hear the news?" she said. "The dead girl's jewelry has been stolen."

I decided to question Aubry. He was in the office. When I entered, he gave orders to one of the officers.

"Keep everyone out of here!" he shouted.

"Who is 'everyone'?" I inquired.

"Everyone," the Commissioner said wryly, "except you and Atwell."

I wondered if my exclusion wasn't due to the fact that I was, at that moment, his interlocutor. In any case, the order had a calming effect on me: it warded off the imminent danger that all of us in the hotel—except the victim—would become detectives. The Commissioner offered me a cigarette and proceeded to explain the facts to me.

"Miss Emilia came to me first thing in the morning with the news that her sister's jewelry had been stolen. I told her to stay calm, that Atwell had taken charge of the jewels. Atwell and I had planned that. When I saw him, I asked him about the matter. He admitted to me that after talking to me he had completely forgotten. I have questioned some people; the only ones left are you, Doctor Cornejo and the typist. I believe I am correct that the jewels were in the victim's room until that boy showed up. Nobody has seen them since. But the most interesting thing remains to be said. I gave the order for them to search the deceased's room and... guess what we found?"

He showed me a handwritten piece of paper. I read:

For Mary:
I have to talk to you. I'll wait for you at siesta time, in the hallway. Thank you.
Thank you very much.
CORNEJO

The words *I have to talk to you* brought to my mind an uncomfortable memory. I think I blushed.

After several bold statements, adduced gravely, almost with sadness, the Commissioner continued:

"Cornejo and the typist are in the dining room. The woman's statement is of interest to me. She was in the room shortly after the scene with the boy."

At that moment an officer entered in an agitated state:

"Doctor Cornejo is dead," he announced.

27

WE WENT INTO THE DINING ROOM.

The future will belong to politicians, to the literati, to the educator who controls the rhetoric of detail. There is always a particular detail whose alteration paves the way for the most radical change of the whole. The fact that a person was lying down on the floor of that room, which was so big and empty, was enough to create an image of profuse chaos.

Manning came over to me.

"He's been poisoned," he said.

Doctor Montes, on his knees beside Cornejo's prone body, patted his vest searching for his watch. Atwell and the typist looked on.

"Bring my bag," stammered my colleague, in a drunken voice.

"I'll bring it right away," answered Manning, and he diligently disappeared.

Just at that moment I remembered that Manning, in accordance with the Commissioner's information, was supposed to be incommunicado.

Cornejo's condition was not serious. Regarding the attempted murder, I reached these conclusions: 1) the drug used was not the same as in the previous case; 2) there had been a mistake in the dosage. This could suggest a new guilty party, or that the guilty party did not know the properties of the new drug.

Manning was still not back.

Mentally, I scrutinized the persons in the hotel and wondered to whom to attribute that error. I encountered too many candidates. Thinking of some of them gave me the chills.

"Why is Manning taking so long?" Atwell exclaimed impatiently. "I'm going to get the bag."

Aubry's serious and stunned expression followed him to the door.

"At this rate we'll be left alone," the drunkard remarked.

Aubry didn't respond. At that moment I began to doubt his efficacy.

Atwell came back with the bag, and explained:

"It was on Montes's bed. I can't understand why Manning couldn't find it."

"Perhaps the problem now will be finding Manning," Montes replied.

The gods, who are not ignorant of the future, usually speak through the mouths of children and madmen. I also understand that they favor alcoholics.

My colleague opened the bag, and while he looked for caffeine, he discovered that he was missing a tube of barbiturates.

I admit that for a moment I looked upon Doctor Montes with some suspicion and wondered if, in his drunken state, he was not in part pretending. But now

I must make an incredible statement: when I looked directly into Montes's half-closed eyes, I caught a suspiciously jocular twinkle.

I didn't dilly-dally with details. Again I thought about Cornejo's case. Veronal, a barbiturate, is the erroneous weapon of those who dream the moderate madness of love and don't want to waste the fruits of a tragic death.

And now a prudent hand emerged, like a terrifying conjecture, not erroneous, measuring the dose of the narcotic. Cornejo's hand.

History highlights personalities that have grown because of the defects of others. I had the sensation that all of Aubry's past deficiencies aggrandized Atwell. Can I say, as a symbol of my feelings, that I looked at the black face of my antimagnetic watch, and that I mentally imprinted the exact time the great detective entered upon the scene? I will only add that this reminds me of Parolles's assertion that merit is seldom attributed to whomever it corresponds. "Is it not monstrous?" as Hamlet wonders, in his monologue.

Atwell ordered:

"We have to go out to look for Miguel and Manning. One of the two has taken the jewels. He shouldn't be given time to hide them forever."

The Commissioner looked at him with interest.

"In this sandstorm you can't see more than six feet ahead of you," he observed. "We won't be able to do anything."

"We haven't done anything yet," replied Atwell. "And

allow me to tell you that your 'rigorous' incommunicado isolation of the suspects has not produced results.
I suggest an elementary measure: order a guard to lock
them all up in a room." Atwell addressed me: "Doctor
Huberman, do you consider that Doctor Cornejo's condition requires your attention?"

I didn't know what to say. I opted for the truth.

"I don't think so," I said.

"We will form, then, two committees," Atwell ordered. "We have to carry weapons in case the fugitives
resist. Commissioner Aubry, with an officer, will advance toward the northwest and will then turn in a fan
motion toward the south. Doctor Huberman and I will
first go in the direction of southeast, then we will turn
toward the west. It's now 10:20. Let's try to be back in
the hotel before 5 p.m. Those who have glasses, please
take them."

The Commissioner himself must have felt Atwell's
unassailable superiority. The plan was accepted without
protest.

I went down to my room. I put on my beret, my
specs, the scarf that Aunt Carlota knitted for me, my
peacoat. I remembered our bivouac in Martinez, my
years as a boy scout; the canteen bulged in one of my
pockets; in the other, a packet of crackers.

28

WE WENT OUT INTO A MURKY BRIGHTNESS, devoid of both background and sky, amid gusts and spirals of sand, an empty and abstract world where all objects had disintegrated, where the air was almost thick, harsh, burning, painful. I walked stooped over as if seeking an invisible tunnel through which to ford the windstorm, groping, squinting, trying not to lose my companion.

I thought—alas, too late!—that it would have been wise to cross those shifting and raised heaps of sand joined by a rope, like mountain climbers.

By means of rapid-fire synthesis—any form of analysis was, at that moment, not feasible—I gleaned that I was in an unknown and hostile environment, facing problems and dangers I had not been brought up to handle, and that I should, without vacillating, place myself blindly in the hands of my companion. My only concern was to follow him—to where, I didn't even ask myself. I applied myself to overcoming my immediate resistance, forgetting all notion of goal or purpose. My destiny, as I thought of it at that moment, was to wander in an uncertain world. I wasn't even afraid that we would get lost; I was only afraid of losing Atwell.

"Wait here. I'll be back in a second," Atwell shouted.

I stood up straight. I was next to a solid white wall. Atwell had vanished.

My obscured vision and a perplexity influenced by recollections of *L'Atlantide* and of having dreamed of similar experiences elevated those white plains into a disproportionate and labyrinthine architecture. I looked more circumspectly. There were a few stone steps, a green door. I recognized the New East End Hotel.

Why had Atwell not wanted me to go with him? Asking me to wait for him inside would not have constituted an excessive show of courtesy. I had an uncontrollable impulse: to go up the steps two at a time, and knock on the door. I didn't move. I had taken on the dangerous attitude of someone who has forsworn all responsibility, who has given himself over to the will of another. I didn't dare to disobey Atwell's orders.

Until then I had been aware only of peripheral sensations: the sand against my skin, my clothes whipped by the wind. Now from deep down in my chest radiated a slow intense burn of humiliation and resentment.

I continued waiting. Finally Atwell returned.

"Why did you leave me outside?" I asked abrasively.

"What did you say?"

Since nothing would now spare me the suffering I had endured, repeating the question was exasperating.

"I went to get my gun," replied Atwell.

This was not the explanation I sought. Did the wind force him to answer me in this manner? Or some secret worry...?

I must have walked some fifty meters following Atwell before I understood what his words implied: the
possibility—the only possibility I could then imagine—
of getting entangled in a shooting match with Manning, which was not a pleasant thought.

We continued dragging ourselves through the sand,
fighting the wind, until we reached an area where there
were dark patches of esparto grass, where the consistency of the ground had changed—it now felt like
muddy soil—where the storm was less murky, less
severe. We paused. Gusts of two distinct smells were
blowing: the more immediate one smelled damp and
muddy; another, airier, seemed to come from something huge that was rotting. Atwell put one foot forward, tapping the ground to see if it was solid.

"We'll have to go around the esparto bushes," he
said.

He moved ahead cautiously. I followed him. I remembered the story of the pharmacist's horse that Esteban had told us.

I didn't think that I could lose Atwell, or that Manning, a stranger and a criminal, could leap out from
behind a bush. Sinking into the mud was the danger
with which I was obsessed. We continued walking. At
no moment did I wonder in which direction we were
going, nor where the hotel was; all this was incumbent
upon my companion.

I thought I saw a spider in the mud. Then another,
and then many. They were crabs. I thought that if I fell,
I would fall face down, in a swimming position. But

then my face would sink into the mud and the crabs would be moving at the level of my eyes. It might be better to fall over backwards. Then I imagined the terror of knowing I was being assaulted by the timid, obstinate, multiple legs of invisible crustaceans.

We went around the last esparto bushes; we heard, mixed in with the screaming wind, a furious and distant sea, and before us opened the most horrendous and desperate vision: a black, slimy, endless beach quivering with crabs. "The bad part of seeing a spectacle like this," I thought, "is that later one will surely find it again in hell."

I tried to make out the sea along the horizon. I saw a promontory in the crab bed, something that looked like a boat dragged in by the current.

"What is it?" I asked.

"A whale," he shouted.

I smelled the putrefaction, and imagined the enormous carcass of the whale, being swarmed and devoured by crabs.

"Let's go back. We've got to continue searching."

We went into the dark labyrinth of bushes. Atwell was walking too swiftly. Two or three times I had to ask him to wait for me. I was stopping continually, to test the ground. I didn't want to die in that desolate place.

With suppressed joy I saw that Atwell was waiting for me. I came up to him.

"Did you hear that?" he asked.

Something in the tone of his voice startled me.

"I didn't hear anything," I answered sincerely.

"He must be somewhere around here." He took a black revolver out of his pocket. "Let's go."

"I'll wait for you."

A mysterious numbness invaded my arms and legs. Atwell went around a bush and disappeared. I tried to shout. Then I thought that if I shouted I'd put Manning on his guard. Or had I simply lost my voice? Then I shouted. I realized immediately that no one would answer me. No one answered me. I ran without remembering the spongy danger I was skirting. I went around that esparto bush. I reached the place where I should have found Atwell. He wasn't there.

There was a dead calm. I didn't know when it had begun. I wondered if this was the end of the storm or just a break. The light was greenish and at times mauve. It didn't correspond to any particular time of the day.

I shouted again. Nobody answered. I tried to retrace my steps, to return to the place where Atwell left me. I wasn't sure if I was in the same spot. All the bushes looked alike. I sat on the ground.

I didn't know how much time had passed, but Atwell's disappearance had been too sudden. I wondered if he was hiding.

Then I asked myself a more important question: Why had I, having adopted as a fundamental rule of conduct never to expose myself to danger, never having signed any protest against any government, having favored the appearance of order over order itself, if in order to impose it violence would be required, having allowed people to step all over my ideals, in order not to defend them; why had I, having aspired only to be a private citizen and, in the lap of luxury of my private life, find the "hidden path" and refuge against dangers both external and within; why had I—I again exclaimed— involved myself in this preposterous story and followed Atwell's senseless orders? To bribe fate, I swore that if I got back alive to the hotel I would benefit from the lesson and never again allow vanity, sycophancy or pride to induce me to act without premeditation.

If I wanted Atwell to find me, I shouldn't move. But would it be a good thing for Atwell to find me? Why had he disappeared? Why had he hidden? This esparto bush was doubtlessly the one I had wanted to find. This was the set place, the place where my enemies knew they could find me, where, without any risk, they could kill me.

I wanted to run away. I stayed there. Any movement was dangerous. Right now I wasn't too far from the sand of the hotel. Going from one bush to another might move me irremissibly further into that labyrinth of vegetation and mud.

Controlling my fear, I faced the possibility of spending the night in the crab bog. I thought of the animals who prowled around there: cats, agile and perverse; herds of wild boar; and—when the wind ceased—birds of prey that would peck at me, confusing me with carrion. I imagined my body lying in the mud, asleep, on a moonless night. That mud was a moving weave of crab legs.

I had to protect myself from the whimsical combinations of my imagination. I had to wait, calmly. But how long had I already waited? I felt too impatient to look at my watch. I walked in any direction, almost without taking care to sidestep the bushes, stooping because the windstorm was getting worse. Suddenly, I thought I could again feel the sand on my face. I started to run, lost my footing, fell in the mud. When I stood up, wet and trembling, the wind whipping my face carried no trace of sand.

I felt that I was about to lose control over my nerves. I'm a doctor. I'm not unaware of symptoms. I resorted to my flask of rum.

The next thing I remember of that horrible afternoon, I was walking without knowing where, tired, continually falling down, now used to the touch of the crabs, guided by a minimum of consciousness. I thought I saw in the distance, through an opening in the esparto bushes, the broad expanse of sand. When, finally, I reached the last bush, I found I was again on the crab beach, with the sound of the sea in the distance and the carcass of the whale. I was in the place where Atwell and I had started out. I had followed the fatal circle that disoriented men follow to the left and animals to the right (or the other way around: I don't remember).

I think I cried. I think there was a suspension of my consciousness, as if beyond despair I had found sleep or stupefaction. Afterwards I felt a slight sensation of warmth. I opened my eyes. My hand seemed to radiate a purplish halo. I looked at the sky. My indifferent eyes contemplated a feeble and remote sun.

Impulsively I consulted my watch. It was 4:35 p.m. I looked at the sun, and at the sea. With renewed hope, I turned north.

29

EXHAUSTED, BRUISED, COVERED WITH DRY mud and sand, my eyes burning, my head aching and congested, I made it to the hotel. I had managed to overcome the hardships of the walk, heartened by a single goal: I would not let anything or anybody postpone my hot bath, a witch-hazel massage, the tray of stew with eggs, salads, fruits, and mineral water that Andrea would bring to my bed.

How I had longed for the moment I would find myself beside the entrance to the hotel! To enter, I didn't even have to knock on the door. It opened magically, though the Commissioner was there, with his hand on the doorknob, as well as Montes, welcoming and drunk. With what undeniable and serene conviction that interior and those objects formed part of the magic of which the poet never speaks: the magic of the domestic, of the everyday! I arrived at that hotel like a man who's been shipwrecked boards his rescuing ship, or better yet, like Ulysses, "to his beloved island, to his hearth in Ithaca."

"We'd already decided that you'd run away," asserted Montes.

Again the sand, the crabs, the mud: now in my

fellow man's soul. "The winter wind is not as inclement as your brother's heart."

"Atwell didn't come back with you?" Aubry asked.

"No," I said, "we lost sight of each other. And the boy?"

They hadn't found him. I asked about Manning.

"Here I am," the latter replied.

He waved his pipe in greeting and smiled good-naturedly, amid a rain of ashes.

I hurried to answer:

"I never suspected you."

These words, brilliant and opportune in my conversation with Montes, were surprising to Manning. Barely concealing his reaction, he raised his eyebrow and looked at me glumly.

"The storm will pass," affirmed the doctor, going over to the window. "I see a seagull."

Manning intervened:

"What are your plans?"

I thought he was speaking to me. I was ready to declare "a bath, a massage," etc., when the Commissioner responded:

"To recover the jewelry."

While the others argued—carrying on in their perplexity, ignorance, poverty of imagination—I was receiving an inspiration. A dilemma presented itself to me: pleasures or duty. I didn't hesitate.

"I know where the jewelry is," I said, stressing each syllable. "I know who the criminal is."

The effect of this declaration exceeded my most

optimistic expectations. The Commissioner lost his composure, Manning, his impenetrability, Montes, his drunkenness. The three of them looked at my mouth as if they were waiting for the judgment of God to be pronounced.

"The criminal is the boy," I finally announced. "He felt an unhealthy passion for Mary, and resentment, and fear of being exposed..."

"Do you have any proof?" asked the Commissioner.

"I know where the jewels are," I replied, triumphantly. "Follow me."

I walked ahead of them resolutely, and somewhat pompously. Now preceded, now followed by our shadows, we went down the stairs. We went along the dark hallway. We reached the room where the trunks were kept.

"A match," I demanded.

We lit the candle. I pointed resolutely ahead with my index finger.

"There are the jewels."

The Commissioner lifted up the bird.

"Too light," he pronounced, shaking his head. "Straw and feathers."

Before I could recover, an indisputable pocketknife opened the bird's chest. The Commissioner was right.

I will always register my defeats and my victories with equanimity. May nobody call me an unreliable narrator.

My error—if this can be called an error—does not offend me. An ignorant person wouldn't have committed it. I am a *literato*, a reader, and as often occurs with men of my class, I confused reality with a book. If a book speaks to us about an embalmed bird, and then the disappearance of certain jewels, what other hiding place would the author resort to without appearing ridiculous?

30

I DON'T THINK THAT MY INTERVENTION CAN be called a failure; I did not feel annoyance or shame, or resentment. I felt, only, an urgent need to brush the mud off myself and sink into a hot tub of water, to nourish myself with salads and fruits, on a soft mattress, horsehair pillows and clean sheets.

Astutely I said:

"Gentlemen, let's go into the dining room."

With this semblance of an invitation I walked them over toward Andrea's habitat. My veiled purpose was to order my cousin to make dinner.

When my companions had taken their seats around the narrow dining table, Aubry looked at us somberly and stated:

"I am pleased to see us all gathered in the aperitif section."

As for me, I gave in to an unforgiveable weakness: I sat down. I thought that after that utterance I couldn't withdraw. (I thought: "I'll stand up in a few minutes.") Immediately the typist came in with the bottles and wine glasses, and Manning began to speak.

Some people are immune to the experiences of others. Manning was one of them. With irritation I heard him assert that he knew the truth about Mary's death.

Nevertheless, I must admit that his explanation

didn't begin, as might have been expected, with more or less sarcastic allusions to a companion-in-arms who had been led astray by literary imagination... Urbanity or prudence?

"I already explained to these gentlemen," began Manning, indicating the Commissioner and Montes, "that I went over to the New East End Hotel to look for a book. Here it is."

He took out of his pocket a book with an angular design of green, purple, black and white on the cover. Puzzled, we passed it around, silently. I think I remember that the author was English, Phillpotts.

"Read on page twenty the marked paragraph," Manning continued.

The Commissioner put on his tortoiseshell eyeglasses, and, moving his finger faster than his eye, he read Mary's letter in a loud and hesitant voice, her interrupted farewell. But now it was a long letter, with details that didn't correspond to Mary, Atwell, and Emilia, which ended on page twenty-one with the words "your grateful friend" signed by someone named BEN.

"What does this mean?" asked Aubry.

"It means," replied Manning, "that Inspector Atwell took home one of the novels translated by Miss Mary."

Then he was silent, as if waiting for his words to obliterate us.

"Let us recapitulate," he then said. "On the eve of the murder two incidents occur that doubtlessly convince the criminal that the moment to act has come. On the beach Atwell becomes angry because Mary insists upon taking a swim despite the fact that the ocean is rough. For the detectives this argument would be an indication that Atwell did not want Mary to die. Let's look now at the rescue. Emilia saves Mary. So then Emilia doesn't want Mary to die. Another deduction the judicious detective expects: Cornejo (who had given Mary his consent for her to go swimming) is a possible, though not yet credible, suspect. But even with all these arguments one can still contend that we don't have any proof that Mary was in danger. She herself denied it. Cornejo, an expert in winds and tides, judged that it wasn't dangerous to take a swim. The possibility that Emilia and Atwell were accomplices has been insinuated. I, however, do not believe that Emilia is involved in the crime. In that nautical episode she was, perhaps, Atwell's unintentional instrument. The movements of a person fighting waves so as to avoid death by drowning can appear, even to someone watching from nearby, playful displays of happiness, and the opposite is also true. Atwell had created a general state of apprehension with regards to Mary's swim. Afterwards, when he shouted, as the girl was swimming out to sea, 'She can't get back in,' nobody doubted him. Nostalgia for melodrama; the feeling that life, even when adventurous, doesn't fully satisfy; a desire for cooperation that proclaims, beyond differences and antagonisms, the secret brotherhood of man, prevent us from easily rejecting any message about a fellow human being in danger. Doctor Huberman himself, whom it doesn't seem wise to exclude from the list of suspects and to consider as an impartial witness, thought that Mary was drowning."

"And to think that we believed Manning was the future solitaire champion..." sighed Doctor Montes.

"Let's take a close look now," continued Manning, "at the after-dinner discussion, which ended with Emilia stepping out into the night. Atwell seemed calm and conciliatory; Emilia, offended by Mary. Normally these signs would corroborate for the detectives their favorable opinion of Atwell and would make them suspect, at some moment, the girl."

Aubry looked at him with astonishment, tossed two pieces of cheese and three olives into his mouth, then downed a glass of vermouth. Manning continued:

"Now we arrive at the moment of Mary's death. The Commissioner has pointed out that even if the Inspector had no lack of motives—he has the same as Miss Emilia—he lacked the opportunity. The death occurred toward dawn, at a time when Atwell was not in this house: he was sleeping in his room at the New East End Hotel. I dare to assert that this argument can be recommended more for its brilliance than its consistency. If the crime had been committed with a firearm, the Commissioner would be right, but in this case poison has been used. When he went downstairs with Cornejo to look for Emilia, Atwell could have easily put the poison in the cup of hot chocolate that was on the night table."

"As I already said, Commissioner," Montes interrupted, "you were so pleased with establishing distinctions between motives and opportunities that you forgot about the case at hand."

I was definitive:

"The Commissioner's distinctions are sound." I declared.

"When Atwell," Manning continued, "discovered that page in the translation (perhaps only a draft) of Phillpotts's book, he understood that he had within reach the 'proof' that would allow him to kill with impunity. Later, the night of the crime, he left the page on the table, beside the manuscript of Mary's new translation; that same night, or the next morning, he took the book out of her library, so that no one could prove that Mary's message was, simply, a paragraph from a novel. I discovered the sheet of paper on the table; Atwell had certainly succeeded in making this discovery inevitable. I admit that while I read those handwritten lines with an understanding that was still imperfect, I felt deeply moved. I believed I was glimpsing the modest shining of the truth, perhaps glimpsing, also, my victory in the investigation. I spoke with Atwell. He didn't seem excited about my theory: in order to excite him, I became enthusiastic. He said he didn't want to get personally involved in the whole matter, but that he would try to help me. He brought me an English novel that the girl had been translating at the time of her death; I read it; between the two of us we both read the novels she had already translated. Atwell had influenced my thinking and I thought and acted in accordance with his insights. However, because of who knows what naïve egoism on his part, he made a mistake: he thought that my thinking would come to a halt when he reached a definite (and for him, favorable) interpretation of the problem. It didn't come to a halt."

I remembered the spider that Manning had placed on the window and the web it had woven in three days. Manning continued:

"I think I understand Atwell's plan: some signs, not many, could suggest Emilia's guilt; when the police, in their eagerness to capture the guilty party, were satisfied with these suppositions and ready to detain the girl, he, indirectly, would make the 'proofs' of the suicide appear. He counted on the detectives seeing that solution as definitive. In fact, they would reach it laboriously, then accept it enthusiastically and abandon, out of a lack of interest, any other hypothesis. But he hadn't counted on the astute methods of Commissioner Aubry: fabricating the proof by means of a severe interrogation. This, and the firm decision the Commissioner made to charge Emilia, made those reflexive and ambitious projects misfire. The man wasn't very scrupulous: to get out of an uncomfortable situation—he was having an affair with his fiancée's sister—he had resort to murder; but now, because of his guilt, he couldn't allow them to torture and perhaps condemn Emilia. From that moment on he acted nervously, depending on the circumstances provided by chance. Let me give as an example the stealing of the jewelry. There was no such robbery. It was staged by Atwell to suggest another guilty party. (Emilia had no reason to steal those jewels: she would inherit them.) Atwell ran the risk of the investigation coming up with the hypothesis of two felons: a murderer and a thief. But those of us gathered here are few, and the idea of there being a criminal amongst us is already astonishing; if someone were to prove that there were two, we wouldn't believe him. When Cornejo discovered the boy with the dead woman, Atwell took advantage of the occasion. He thought, perhaps, that the boy's soul was already monstrous, so he could easily attribute to him an additional monstrosity. I understand, but I do not forgive him. Thus I, who do not belong to the police force, offer these explanations that may damn him. Perhaps I seem like an intruder and a raging fool, but we shouldn't forget that Atwell speculated about the child's pathological sensibility, about his tendency to run away, about his passions and fears. Perhaps the best that can be said about Atwell is that, in his desperation to save the woman he loved, he acted rashly. This also explains the attempt on Cornejo's life. The typist had entered Mary's room after the scene of the kiss and before Atwell could take the jewels and declare that Miguel had stolen them. When the Commissioner was ready to take down statements from Doctor Cornejo and the typist, Atwell tried to eliminate the former. By doing this he would draw our attention away from the typist and make us think that Cornejo was the important witness. Upon judging these actions let us not be too severe with Atwell. His intention was to put Cornejo to sleep, not to kill him. As to the latter's note to Mary, there's not much to add. Atwell

discovered it, hid it prudently away (that's why the police didn't find it during their first search), and when
he wanted to foment confusion and plant false clues,
he again put it in Mary's room. But let's go on with the
story. When Atwell understood that I had taken advantage of a pretext to leave the hotel, he guessed the truth.
He immediately organized the rescue missions and, accompanied by Doctor Huberman, he headed toward
the New East End. There he confirmed that Phillpotts's
book was missing, the book that would allow it to be
proven that Mary's message was, simply, a paragraph
from her translation. Perhaps he took advantage of the
excursion to take the jewelry. Perhaps we crossed paths
in the sand. The storm saved me. I submit that had he
caught me, he'd have killed me, and then accused me of
having murdered his girlfriend."

Doctor Montes asked:

"What reason would Atwell have had for killing
Mary?"

Commissioner Aubry looked at him very wide-eyed.

"Reasons for homicide are never lacking," he replied. "Doctor Huberman, right here, sketched in his
statement a suggestive portrait of Miss Mary. It is not
the first time a man has been in love with one woman
and dominated by another."

As if Manning had in his hands the invisible Book
of Destiny, I asked him where Atwell was. He answered
with indifference:

"Either fleeing, or committing suicide, among the
crabs."

31

MUSCARIUS—OUR DISHEVELED AND OBESE typist—entered the room, in thrall to the audible flight of a horsefly. She announced mechanically:

"La Bruna, the owner of the other hotel, wants to speak with the Commissioner."

Before she retreated, the Commissioner ordered her to show Mr. La Bruna in.

La Bruna looked a little like Wagner, but somewhat younger. He was wearing a pajama jacket and loose trousers the color of café au lait. He handed Aubry a package, and said:

"Today at noon, Inspector Atwell asked me to give you this. Forgive me for not bringing it earlier. There was so much wind that it was impossible to go out."

"Where is the Inspector?" asked Aubry.

"I don't know," replied La Bruna. "He gave me this and left. I told him not to go out in the storm, but I saw in his eyes that I'd be wise to keep silent."

Aubry withdrew with the package. We didn't know what to talk about. I attempted a remark about the weather. La Bruna predicted that the weather would improve that very night. We said goodbye and he left.

The Commissioner returned. He looked at each of

us one by one, with sad and scrutinizing eyes, as if he were expecting to uncover a secret. He asked:

"Do you know what Atwell sent me?"

"The jewels," replied Manning.

He was right. I thought it opportune to add:

"Atwell didn't send them. They are not real jewels. Mr. La Bruna is not Mr. La Bruna. This is merely a bogus ploy on the part of Manning, to convince us."

Faced with a severe look from the Commissioner, Manning blushed. I thought that those stones and those pieces of metal were more eloquent than any written message.

Montes asked the Commissioner:

"What are you going to do now?"

"Give the jewels to Miss Emilia. Give them to her personally."

For my part, I would try not to miss that meeting.

"I'm going to take a bath and change," I said.

With what impatience had I been waiting for that bath, that paradise via immersion! However, upon articulating these words, I had already postponed it once again.

32

I SETTLED INTO MY OBSERVATION POST, AT the dark end of the hallway, facing Mary's room.

Suddenly I regretted this bold gesture. What fatal flaw compelled me to get mixed up in this affair? Why was I exposing myself in this final stage, when I already saw myself miraculously free of annoyances and commitments? Why was I allowing an unhealthy curiosity to separate me from Petronius, literature, celluloid? I found the answer. I'm a tireless observer of humankind, and in my eagerness to scrutinize traits, reactions, and idiosyncrasies, I am prepared to put up with discomforts and to face dangers.

Commissioner Aubry silently appeared in the opening of the staircase and walked toward my hiding place. He was carrying the package of jewels in his right hand. He stopped. If he had reached out his hand he would have touched me. He knocked on the door. Emilia opened. I saw the Commissioner from the back, and Emilia facing toward me.

"Here are the jewels," the Commissioner said, and he gave her the package.

There was a subdued hint of elation in Emilia's eyes; the Commissioner continued:

"They've been sent by your fiancé."

"Did he find them?"

"He didn't find them. He's returning them."

Emilia looked at him, perplexed.

"This remittance amounts to a confession," the Commissioner explained, brutally. "Atwell killed Miss Mary. My men are looking for him in the crab bogs as we speak. I hope they find him alive."

"You're lying to me!" Emilia cried out, and I felt hysteria overtaking me. "He's already dead. He did it to save me. You must believe me: it was to save me. I'm the guilty party, for everything."

Afterwards there was a commotion during which the Commissioner was trying to calm Emilia, then a long conversation in a persuasive tone, then an almost friendly farewell. The Commissioner came out into the hallway, closed the door, and walked away with a firm step.

I was still motionless, tense. How much time had passed? Maybe ten minutes. Maybe a half hour. In the dead girl's room something fell, heavily. My hand, white and tremulous, took hold of the doorknob. Before opening I knew what I would find. Emilia's body was lying on the floor. On the table was a vial. On the label I read the word *Strychnine.*

33

WE GREETED THE DAWN AFTER A NIGHT OF exertion and high anxiety, gathered again in the dining room, smoking, drinking coffee, listening to the Commissioner's harsh proclamation.

"Atwell has carried out all the actions that Manning has laid at his door," Aubry finally summarized, "except one: he did not kill Miss Mary. From the start he realized that Emilia was the culprit. In order to save her, he was clumsy, unscrupulous, even heroic. He didn't hesitate to vilify a child. He didn't hesitate—when all appeared lost and he tried to convince us of his own guilt—to commit suicide. But now there is no doubt: Emilia committed the crime. She attempted to take her own life with the poison we searched for in every corner of the house, with the poison that killed Miss Mary."

On the table was Mary's suitcase, the same suitcase Atwell had inspected the evening I spied on him from the darkened hallway. The Commissioner opened it and handed each of us a stack of handwritten pages. I leafed through mine (I cleverly made off with them and keep them as a souvenir); some, numbered consecutively, contain chapters of novels; others, paragraphs or just sentences (sometimes repeated, with variations and corrections). For example, on one page I read: *I took off my stockings*, and a little lower down, the corrected version: *I took off my socks.* Another page read: *But four days after I arrived there, a man arrived,* and further down: *a man came* (which is proof of Mary's fine ear and rich vocabulary). Aubry told us:

"One of these minutes was the dead girl's 'message.' The Inspector, who knew her well, knew that the young lady kept all the copies of her translations. When he realized that his fiancée was in a compromised situation, he remembered the dead girl's compulsion, recalled the letter in the English novel by Phillpotts and looked for the drafts in her suitcase. He was lucky, and it was to be expected, because the Inspector is an intelligent man."

Presently, one of Aubry's policemen came into the dining room. He had dark circles under his eyes and was covered with mud. The night before he had accompanied the other policeman and the chauffeur, for whom the crab bogs held no secrets, in search of the Inspector. They found him asleep next to an esparto bush. The Inspector had counted on a few hours of freedom. In that space of time it was easier to get lost and tired and fall asleep in the crab bog, than to cross it or die there. Now Atwell was awaiting us in the office. I didn't want to see him, but I was glad he was alive. Very soon I would give him my permission to see his fiancée, who was already out of danger. The presence of a doctor in that hallway, beside that door, had been providential. A few more minutes and a life blossoming with hopes would have been cut short. The tragedy had paralyzed my brain; but my hands, my obedient professional hands, had administered emetics to induce vomiting.

I breathed deeply and felt my chest expand with immense pride and timid joy. I promised myself, resolutely, the hot bath, the change of clothing, and breakfast. With an alert spirit I greeted the morning, not with the contrite fatigue resulting inevitably from a sleepless night, but rather with the joy and faith of a pleasurable awakening.

34

THE NEXT MORNING WE MOVED THE DINING
room table against one of the windows, and the Commissioner, Montes and I had breakfast while keenly
staring at the sandy beach, the tamarisk bushes, the
New East End Hotel, the pharmacy, the sky—which
all formed again, after the endless storm, an orderly
world, shining serenely in the sunlight, like an enormous flower.

I was having the breakfast from my periods of intense literary work—black tea, hard-boiled eggs, toast
and honey—when I saw in the lion-colored expanse of
sand a slight man in a blue sweater and light gray trousers approaching us.

We were so busy arguing about who the little man
could be, and who saw farther, mountain men, plains-
men, or seamen, and even about what was the farthest
distance human sight could reach, that we were surprised by the news that someone had arrived at the
hotel.

"It's the pharmacist," Esteban explained. "He wants
to talk to the Commissioner."

"Have him come in," the latter said, and stood up.

The pharmacist—in the blue sweater and light gray

trousers—entered the dining room. He was a poker-faced man, with swollen eyes and a smooth complexion; when he made any movement he sighed, as if the inevitable waste of energy were worrisome. He greeted us parsimoniously and began a laborious conversation with Aubry in one corner of the room. Then he took a letter out of his pocket. Aubry read it nervously.

The two men sat down at our table. Aubry ordered Esteban:

"A cup of coffee for Señor Rocha." He then addressed the latter: "Did you know him from before? The day he went to see you, did he seem normal?"

"No, not normal. But, as you know, he was strange."

"Crazy?"

"I wouldn't go that far. He was intelligent, or rather, studious."

"Why do you say 'was'?" Aubry asked. "I am not sure that he's dead."

"I'm not sure either. However, I think it's likely."

"When did you notice that he had stolen the poison?"

"I told your officer the truth. I haven't sold any strychnine for years."

"But why didn't you verify whether you had the bottle?"

Paulino Rocha gently lowered his eyes.

"I noticed it the other day. You know, life in the country..."

"Why didn't you come right away to give me the news?"

"I have a susceptible throat, and with the wind-storm... When the letter arrived I came right away. Of course, by then the storm was already over."

This system of questions and answers, this enig-matic catechism, was beginning to exasperate me. Aubry's poor manners, and the pharmacist's as well, which excited our sincere curiosity, made me angry. I hesitated over several efficient interventions, any one of which would have overcome Aubry's resistance and obliged him to show us the letter. I asked him:

"Why don't you show us that letter?"

As his whole answer he gave it to me. I read the fol-lowing lines, written in pencil, with a firm and imper-sonal handwriting:

Señor Paulino Rocha,
Farmacia Los Pinos,
Bosque del Mar

Dear friend:
You will be surprised by the reason for this let-ter, but you are my only friend and I have behaved very badly with you.
Andrea and Esteban are my aunt and uncle, but I don't love them. They don't even let me kill birds and other animals. You know that I had the albatross hidden among the trunks. They wanted me to be examined by the doctor, but I scared him off right away. He was more skittish than the ot-ters that Dad and I used to embalm.

Did you know the Gutiérrez sisters? I loved them dearly, especially Mary. Now that she's died I don't hold any grudge against her. I loved her so much, and every time I went to give her a kiss she'd get angry, as if it were something bad. She was always nice to me when people were around, but if we were alone, she didn't even want to talk to me. I tried to explain, but she'd get angry.

If I tell you what I did later you're not going to forgive me and I want us to be friends forever. When I went to the pharmacy to look for arsenic for the albatross and for the algae, I stole a bottle of strychnine that was on the middle shelf, under the clock.

The night they all went out to look for Miss Emilia, Mary had gotten very angry with me. I hid in the hallway and when Atwell was going to meet up with the others, to go out looking for Emilia, Mary blocked his path, pushed him away from the light of the staircase and kissed him in such a way that I started crying. I heard her say to him, laughing: "Tomorrow remind me to tell you what happened to me with the kid."

I thought: "I'm going to do something terrible." Now I understand that I did what anyone would have done in my place.

I went down to my room, looked for the strychnine, went to Mary's room and put half of the little bottle into the cup of hot chocolate that she always had before going to bed. I mixed it with the spoon so that the poison would dissolve completely and when I was drying it off I heard Mary's footsteps. While I was escaping, I dropped the bottle. I didn't have time to pick it up. I went out through Emilia's room.

The next day I returned to look for the bottle, but it wasn't there. I wanted to take the strychnine, just as Mary had.

I would have explained everything to the Commissioner in order to avoid unpleasantness for Emilia, but I can't talk because I am a child.

You know that I made my little house in the abandoned boat on the beach. I have many bottles of water, biscuits and a little bag of maté in there. The sea is rising with the storm. I'm going to the boat now to wait for the water to carry it away. When you read this letter, the waves and the water will have covered your faithful and little friend.

MIGUEL FERNÁNZEZ

P.S.: Please send the albatross to my parents.

I returned the letter to the Commissioner. In silence I crossed the dining room and peered out of a window facing the sea. Miguel's boat was not on the beach.

Emilia confirmed what Miguel had said about the bottle of strychnine. She found it the morning of Mary's death. She hid it, because from the very first moment she thought that her fiancé was the murderer. For the same reason she made the cup of chocolate disappear.

Of the *Joseph K* and Miguel there was no news. Commissioner Aubry considered that Miguel's letter was sufficient proof and no longer suspected Emilia.

As for me, I have written the pages you've read, because some friends of my mother—the only women friends I have—wanted my role in the investigation to be documented. I protested, said that the part I played was minimal, that I had simply guessed correctly. . . But they insisted, so here I am, apologetic and blushing, putting the *Finis coronat opus* to this chronicle of my unexpected detective adventures.

All that's left for me to add is that Emilia and Atwell have married and, as far as I know, they are happy. At times I wonder about the intimate life of this pair who so often looked at each other believing the other a criminal and yet never ceased to be in love.

THE NEVERSINK LIBRARY

THE NEVERSINK LIBRARY